Spirit Willing

A Savannah Haunting

A Savannah Haunting

A Savannah Haunting

A Savannah Haunting

A Savannah Haunting

Spirit Willing

A Savannah Haunting

Susan B. Johnson

BONAVENTTURE
— books —
SAVANNAH

Bonaventture Books
4602 Sussex Place
Savannah, GA 31405

Other than references to authentic Savannah locales, this is a work of fiction. All the characters were born of the author's imagination, and any resemblance to real people is by pure coincidence.

Jacket photo by Nancy Heffernan
Author photo by Fred A. Johnson

Library of Congress Cataloging-in-Publication Data
Johnson, Susan B. (Susan Belt), 1934-
   Spirit willing : a Savannah haunting / by Susan B. Johnson. -- 1st ed.
      p. cm.
Summary: "Does the ghost of Cyrus Thornheart exist? Or does he live in Olivia's imagination? Set in present-day Savannah, GA, in this ghost story for non-believers, only the reader knows for sure"--Provided by publisher.
   ISBN-13: 978-0-9724224-6-8 (hardcover : alk. paper)
   ISBN-10: 0-9724224-6-3 (hardcover : alk. paper)
   1. Savannah (Ga.)--Fiction. I. Title.

PS3610.O3833S65 2007
813'.6--dc22

                                                2007010315
First Edition, May 2007
Printed in Canada

Acknowledgments

Many thanks are due to author Rosemary Daniell and the members of Zona Rosa, who provided me with an invaluable sounding board when this book was a work-in-progress.

Thanks also to Wayne Smalley for his expert advice and assistance.

But the largest portion of my gratitude goes to my husband, Fred Johnson, for his patience, his encouragement, and his staunch belief in me — if not in Cyrus Thornheart.

For my son and daughter, Tim and Kelly

. . . the spirit indeed is willing, but the flesh is weak.
Matthew 26: 40-41

THORNHEART-WADE FAMILY TREE

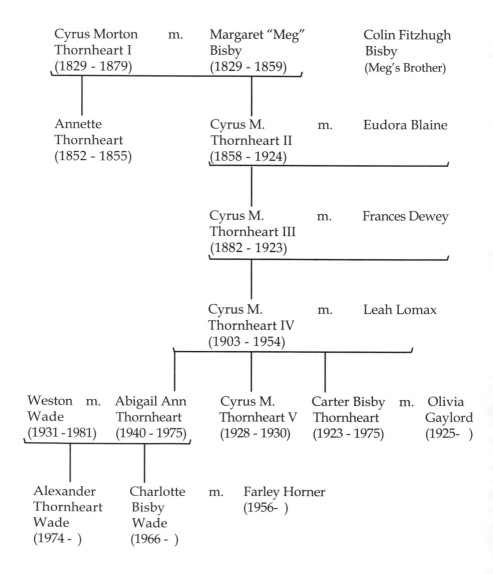

Cyrus Morton Thornheart I (1829 - 1879) m. Margaret "Meg" Bisby (1829 - 1859)

Colin Fitzhugh Bisby (Meg's Brother)

Annette Thornheart (1852 - 1855)

Cyrus M. Thornheart II (1858 - 1924) m. Eudora Blaine

Cyrus M. Thornheart III (1882 - 1923) m. Frances Dewey

Cyrus M. Thornheart IV (1903 - 1954) m. Leah Lomax

Weston Wade (1931 -1981) m. Abigail Ann Thornheart (1940 - 1975)

Cyrus M. Thornheart V (1928 - 1930)

Carter Bisby Thornheart (1923 - 1975) m. Olivia Gaylord (1925-)

Alexander Thornheart Wade (1974 -)

Charlotte Bisby Wade (1966 -) m. Farley Horner (1956-)

August, 1859
Savannah, Georgia

e lifts her hand from the counterpane, cradles it, and studies its pale translucence in the light from the bedside candle. He measures her labored breathing, shallower now and ragged. I'm losing you, he thinks.

Beyond the window he hears the clop-clop of a carriage rumbling down Whitaker Street, sees its lantern bobbing, its driver masked against the yellow death that has stilled the city and sent hundreds of its residents fleeing from the lowlands.

"Cyrus." She struggles against the damp bedclothes, gripping his fingers with surprising force. Fever has enlarged her eyes and sent an unhealthy flush across her brow.

"Cyrus, the baby is crying. You must bring her to me."

"You're dreaming again, Meg. Dreaming."

With his left hand he brushes the limp hair from her forehead, willing his own strength to transfer through his fingers to this woman that he loves. But still she retreats from him, her tide ebbing, her shallow breath now rattling in her chest.

"You must remarry," she whispers.

"Never!" He surprises himself with his vehemence. The mere thought of someone else sharing his life makes him wild with grief and rage.

"And promise me—"

"Hush, love. Go to sleep." He dampens a cloth in the bedside basin and touches it to her parched lips.

She strains toward him, her dark eyes huge with pleading. "Promise you won't ever sell our beautiful house. We've been so happy here. It must always be a home to our children—and to theirs."

"I promise. Now please rest."

At his words she sinks back upon the pillow in exhaustion, hearing neither the sudden lashing of rain against the window nor the clucking of the ormolu clock on the mantle. Peace settles on her thin face as if a circle has been closed, a mission accomplished.

"I love you, Cyrus."

The pale hand trembles, then relaxes, opening like a flower.

March, 2004
Savannah, Georgia

*T*he trouble with you, Charlotte," teased Mary Finn, "is you're so obvious." She plucked the straw from her iced tea and inspected the glass. "You tip your hand by going directly for the jugular. Be a little more devious."

"I don't have time for devious!" snapped Charlotte. She pushed away from the umbrella table and stood up, brushing impatiently at the wrinkles in her tennis whites. "You know better than anyone that the price of real estate in the historic district is starting to soar. And projections show tourism going up and up—ever since John Berendt wrote that book about Savannah. If I am ever going to do something useful with Aunt Olivia's old mausoleum of a house, now is the time!" She glared at a chip in her nail polish. "Besides," she pouted, "she owes me."

"For what?" said Mary Finn. "For stepping up to the plate after your mom died? Seems to me, you and your brother owe *her*."

"Ugh, Alexander," Charlotte snorted. "Don't remind

me." She snatched her bloody mary from the table, then put it back, centering it carefully in its ring of moisture. "I never *could* figure out what that old woman wanted from me. No matter how hard I tried, I always seemed to fall short of the mark."

"That's ancient history," said Mary Finn. "If you ask me, brooding over past injustices, real or imagined, is like back-pedaling. It requires a lot of energy to get you exactly nowhere."

Charlotte tipped her face skyward, closing her eyes against the glare. "Maybe so, but I'm determined to have Hibiscus House. You've got to admit its location right across from the fountain on Forsyth Park is perfect for a B & B. With Farley's construction company doing the remodeling and my flair for interior décor, I could turn it into one of the most prestigious inns in Georgia." Late afternoon shadows dappled her long, tanned legs and deepened the vertical crease between her brows. "Remind me to look into assisted living facilities — the sooner the better."

Her eyes snapped open, and she shook her bracelets to her wrist. "What if Aunt Olivia forgodsake croaks before I can get clear title? For all I know, she's already promised the house, the furniture, the whole caboodle to the A.S.P.C.A!" Even in a temper, Charlotte remained camera ready.

"Isn't Charles Quinn her lawyer?" asked Mary Finn. "Surely he knows if she has a will, or wouldn't he tell you?"

"He's a clam. I tried to get information out of him a couple of weeks ago, but he just said, 'Now, Charlotte,' and changed the subject." She tucked a stray golden strand into her chignon. "However, he did let something slip, which gave me an idea."

"What?"

"His concern for her state of mind." Charlotte perched her sunglasses atop her head and leaned conspiratorially across the table. "As long as I've known Olivia, she's been a little absent-minded — forgetting her own phone number, locking herself out of the house, that sort of thing." She chortled unpleasantly. "About a year ago she put on a new hat and took a cab to a wedding — wearing her bedroom slippers! But Charlie Quinn seems to think that, in the last six months, she's grown even more peculiar. Apparently, she's begun talking to herself — asking questions out loud when there's nobody around as if she expects an answer. She seems to forgodsake *converse* with people who aren't there!" She straightened, emitting an unattractive little snort. "I should be able to work with that somehow."

Mary Finn sipped her iced tea and watched the Keller brothers, bronzed and balding, stroke their lime-green ball back and forth over the net with metronomic precision. One of them — Larry? Jerry? — missed a lob and lifted a finger to his brother. Both men laughed.

"What do you have in mind?" she asked.

Charlotte listened to the thwup-thwup of the game in progress. Few things gave her as much satisfaction as feeling the ball strike dead center on the racquet and watching it slice low over the net out of her partner's reach. Winning was everything. If you could win with grace, so much the better. She draped herself in her aluminum chair and extended her legs.

"I'm not sure yet. But Alexander and I are Aunt Olivia's only two living relatives, and God knows it's no secret she prefers him. After all, I was already eleven when Olivia took us in, whereas Alexander was only three. They're cut from the same bolt — both spacey and impractical with no understanding of the way the world works—not a whit of appreciation for the potential of things." She stirred her bloody mary with the straw, then took a long pull. "If you ask me, both that house and the old woman who lives there have long outlived their usefulness!" She drummed her scarlet nails on the metal tabletop, then rose abruptly.

There's more to this than envy, thought Mary Finn. Something in Charlotte's character was lacking—some fundamental humanness—which left her twisted and untrustworthy like a leg after rickets.

"Don't you think a dotty old lady like Aunt Olivia needs management? Direction? Charles Quinn can be trusted to oversee her legal matters, but family issues are something else. After all, Mary Finn, there have been Wades and Thornhearts in Savannah since the Revolution. We're dealing with history here." Charlotte warmed to her subject. She was pacing again. "Aunt Olivia needs to be counseled by someone both sensible about money and sensitive to the family's history. With Alexander off cloud-gazing in Ireland, that leaves the job up to me." She settled once more in the shade of the umbrella. "Come with me," she said.

"Where?"

"To Hibiscus House."

"Why?"

"One, I need your professional opinion about its state of repair. And two, it'll be fun. We'll drop in on Aunt Olivia and see for ourselves just how barmy the old girl is."

Mary Finn smiled. "And to think I accused you of not being devious."

"We'll take her a little gift—some sherry—get her talking." Charlotte's ice-blue eyes danced. "Maybe we can find out what's in her will."

"I've always loved that old house," said Mary Finn, "always wanted to see what the inside was like."

"Good! How soon can we do it?"

"Don't you think your aunt should be consulted — or at least forewarned?"

"She's always there. What else does she have to forgodsake do?"

"I've got a one o'clock closing on the Bennet's house tomorrow. Then I guess I'm free for the afternoon."

"Perfect. I'll pick you up at four."

Charlotte drained her glass, zipped up her Nike gym bag, and tucked her tennis racquet under her arm. "Don't even *think* about chickening out," she warned, kissing the air beside her friend's cheek.

She crossed the lawn with long, graceful strides and flung her gear in the trunk of her Honda. Then she slipped into the driver's seat and, with a wave, wheeled out of sight.

"You're a real piece of work, Charlotte Horner," said Mary Finn under her breath.

* * *

As she locked the garden gate behind her, Lucy Bates shifted the pinch of snuff tucked behind her lower lip and spat into the azaleas. She hobbled up the flagstone walk and let herself in through the grade entrance door. Miz Livvy had forgotten to lock it again.

"One of these days," she muttered, shaking her head.

The light had burned out in the stairwell leading down to the kitchen level, but Lucy didn't hesitate. She had dusted and mopped and polished every inch of this old house for as long as she could remember; it was as familiar to her as her own. Slipping off her shoes, she set her grocery bag on the kitchen table and began to unpack whole wheat bread, bran flakes, and Campbell's tomato soup. At the bottom was a tin of Copenhagen, which she tucked into her straw tote, then washed her hands at the sink and tied an apron around her middle.

She heard harpsichord music from the parlor upstairs and knew Miz Livvy was listening to the CD player Alexander had given her four years ago on her 75th birthday. She smiled to herself at the thought. That was one sweet boy. She could picture Miz Livvy sitting in the brocade wing chair beside the fireplace with her head back and mouth open, snoring softly.

Lucy turned on the gas under the teakettle and set about making a sandwich for each of them while Tomochichi wound around her ankles, purring loudly.

"How you know I'm about to fetch me some tuna?" she said to the gray-striped cat. "You some kind of mind reader?" She groped in the pantry for a can, not bothering to pull the chain to turn on the light. In the old days the shelves had held glass jars of rhubarb, pickled eggs, and homemade marmalade. Hooks still thrust from the ceiling beams where smoked hams and mesh bags of Vidalia onions had hung throughout the winter. She lifted the lid on the tea tin and breathed deeply of its aroma—a comfortable smell that reassured her of the permanence of things.

When the kettle whistled, she filled the Havilland tea pot and set it on a tray beside two delicate cups and the plate of sandwiches, made the way Miz Livvy liked them—crusts off and cut in triangles.

She cocked her head at the kitchen clock and adjusted her Timex. If she managed it right, she could get Miz Livvy's supper dishes washed and still get home in time to make up the cot in the attic before Jonas arrived, bag and baggage. The old rage began to rise in her throat when she thought of her son being put out of his apartment. But the air was much too sweet today to get all worked up again. Besides, it wouldn't be so bad having Jonas move back home. He could help with the rent and maybe make some repairs around the house. Lord knows, she could keep him busy enough.

"Swing low, sweet cha-a-a-ree-ott" sang Lucy, prodding Tom aside with her toe. Once Jonas got settled in, she'd come on back over here and bring Miz Livvy some of the chicken and dumplings she'd be making for tonight's supper — Jonas' favorite. She'd sit with her a bit, make sure she ate right.

"Comin' for to carry me ho-o-o-me." Jonas hadn't been happy about moving his things up to the third floor, but Aunt Sis had lived in his old second floor bedroom for the past twenty years, and Lucy wasn't about to give up her own room for nobody. If it gets too hot up there, he can sleep downstairs on the sofa, she decided. We'll work it out somehow.

"Us Bateses look after our own," Lucy told the teapot. She spat into the sink and started upstairs with the tray.

*W*hoever saw such an old fool?" said Olivia. She despised the way her fingers fumbled stiffly as she unbuttoned the back of her blouse. Although she had never been a beauty like Lilah Ravenaux or her own mother, she had in her youth been blessed with pretty hands and thick, coppery hair.

"You're a bit thin," she recalled her mother saying, "but that's not to say you won't fill out in time." Elizabeth Gaylord had lifted Olivia's chin with one finger, inspecting her daughter's profile. "Pinch your upper cheeks a bit, dear, to bring up your color. Remember to compose your expression at all times. Too much movement causes lines." She tried her best to suppress a sigh. "Perhaps if you brush your hair one hundred strokes every night and cultivate the graceful gesture, people will concentrate less on your face."

Olivia had brushed one hundred strokes and more, as if an extra fifty could compensate for her rather broad mouth and freckles.

During her sixteenth summer, she and Lilah Ravenaux

had spent hours buffing each other's nails and sewing ecru lace on all their underthings. Even now when the magnolias bloomed across the street in Forsyth Park, the fragrance brought back the magic of that sultry spring, the special feel of moonlight, and the stirrings of womanhood. Close as sisters, the two lazed on the porch swing sharing dreams and secrets, their bright futures shimmering like a mirage on the horizon.

That August, Lilah met Marshall Heywood, and overnight the lifelong closeness between the two girls evaporated.

Olivia felt betrayed, suffering a wound to her pride that had not healed a year later when Lilah's note arrived asking her to be a Christmas bridesmaid. Then Japan attacked Pearl Harbor, causing the lovers to postpone their wedding and Olivia to weep with guilt and relief. She had seen Lilah only once after that — four years later at Marshall's military funeral in Bonaventure Cemetery. Grief and alcohol had broken her, and the two young women had had little left to say.

"Miz Livvy?" called Lucy with a gentle knock. "Supper dishes all done up. You need anything before I go?"

"Come on in, Lucy dear."

"Here, lemme do it." Lucy took the brush and smoothed Olivia's thinning grey hair with gentle strokes. "Was someone on the phone?"

"Oh dear, I must have been talking to myself again," laughed Olivia. She held up her hands, fingers splayed. "Will you just look at these! I hardly recognize them — all speckled by age spots and swollen at the knuckles. How can I ever get my wedding band off?"

"Why you want to do that?"

"I guess I wouldn't. You know, Lucy, when I turned

thirty and still wasn't married, I resigned myself to being a spinster. Most of my friends had children already, and I used to cry myself to sleep thinking I'd never have a baby of my own."

"But then Mr. Carter came along," said Lucy, who had heard it all before.

"I had known Carter Thornheart since I was fifteen, but I never really looked at him until the summer I turned thirty-three. There he was—home on leave and in his uniform sharing a hymnal with his sister Abigail in the balcony of Christ Church. I was in the opposite balcony, trying hard to concentrate on the service, but when our eyes met, I remember feeling like I couldn't breathe."

"And the next week he planted a big one on you."

"Yes, it happened right over there." She pointed across Whitaker Street to Forsyth Park.

"Um-hmm," said Lucy with a surreptitious glance at her watch.

Olivia wandered to the window, lost in thought, while Lucy turned down the bed covers. I can't remember his face, thought Olivia with a pang. Or the exact sound of his voice.

"Eighteen years later his heart attacked him," she said. "Gone, just like that. All that's left of Carter is this wedding band and his portrait out there on the stair wall."

"Climb in now, Miz Livvy. Don't you be catchin' cold." She drew the drapes across all three windows. "How about I make you some cocoa before I leave?"

"No thank you, Lucy dear. You go on home, and I'll see you in the morning." When she heard the click of the outside door, Olivia slipped out of bed and opened the drapes again. She looked across the dark park to the place where the illuminated fountain sparkled and danced as it had for 146 years, thinking again of Carter's kiss, of her wedding gown, and of their stillborn little boy, last of the Thornheart line.

She was still standing there ten minutes later when the telephone rang.

"Miz Livvy?"

"What is it, Lucy?"

"I locked the back door when I left, but I forgot to check the front. You better go down and see."

"I will."

"And then you go on back to bed, hear?"

"Yes, all right. Good night, Lucy."

"Now don't you forget."

On her way back upstairs, Olivia paused to study the four portraits side by side on the landing. The artist had represented Carter's features accurately enough, but he had failed to capture the spark of humor that played behind his eyes. Without it the handsome face was bland, homogenized, containing nothing of the mystery of the man she had loved.

His father, Cyrus Morton Thornheart IV, glared disapprovingly from the frame beside Carter, and next to him, Carter's grandfather and great grandfather, Cyrus III and Cyrus II. The first Cyrus, builder of Hibiscus House, stood uniformed in profile, half turned from the viewer, his left hand resting on the gilded hilt of a sword. Tucked beneath his right arm was his visored hat—a round patent leather top with white and blue plumage surrounded by a band of imitation leopard fur. His was the most interesting face of all, strong and slightly aggressive, projecting an energy diluted in future generations. All four men were prematurely gray; all four wore the same gold signet ring bearing the Thornheart coat of arms.

"You were a dashing rogue, weren't you?" Olivia said to the oldest Cyrus, as she wiped a bit of dust from the frame. "I'll bet you 'fluttered pulses' just like Richard Cory." Her voice echoed hollowly in the parqueted hall.

A moment later she eased into the four poster so as not to disturb Tomochichi and turned out her bedside lamp. Downtown the clock in St. John's bell tower struck eleven. She fell asleep listening to the familiar creaking of the old house and the faint whoosh of traffic heading south on Whitaker Street.

* * *

At four o'clock she heard the word clearly and sat bolt upright in bed.

"Here." Or was it "hear"?

In the dim glow of the street lamp she saw Tomochichi, hackles high and tail tumescent, spring from the bed and scuttle into the hall.

"Who's there?" she croaked, her heart hammering. But only the ormolu clock on the mantle clucked in reply. Fear prickled up her neck as she stretched out her hand toward the lamp switch.

"No bloody light!" commanded a voice from somewhere in the darkness.

Olivia clutched the covers to her chin and stared wide-eyed into the gloom. "Who's in my room?" she asked again in a high voice.

"I'm over here," came the reply. "And it's not your room!"

I'm dreaming, thought Olivia. In another minute I'll wake up and it'll be morning and the cat will be stretched out in a patch of sunlight at the foot of the bed. But the darkness persisted, and her racing pulse confirmed her consciousness. "Who are you?" she asked again. Poor Lucy. Tomorrow morning she'll find my dead body and think I forgot the lock again. But no answer came, only a faint rustling sound from the corner by the door.

"Identify yourself at once," she said firmly, "or I shall telephone the police." She pushed the covers away and edged toward the far side of the bed.

"Be still, woman!" the voice said rudely. "The police will only get in the way."

"In the way of what?" Olivia dared to ask, not at all certain she wanted to know.

"In the way of keeping my promise. You've already given me greater trouble than I ever thought possible. Don't make it even more bloody complicated!"

"I demand to know who you are!" said Olivia. She was offended by his discourtesy and would have stamped her foot had she been standing.

"I am Cyrus Morton Thornheart," boomed the voice, "Captain of the Savannah Volunteer Guards, 1st Regiment, 1st Brigade, 1st Division of the Georgia Militia. And you, Madam, are residing in *my* house and sleeping in *my* bed!"

"That's absurd," snapped Olivia. "Captain Thornheart was my husband's great great grandfather. He's been dead for more than a hundred years!"

"Quite so, Madam, and an untimely death at that. Snatched away before certain — issues could be resolved."

"Don't be impertinent! If you think I'm going to admit I am sitting here talking to a ghost, you have another think coming. I may be old, but I haven't yet lost my mind!" In defiance, Olivia switched on the light and stared blankly around the empty room.

"On the other hand," she whispered, "maybe I have."

"No, Madam, you are quite sane," said the voice, "merely a bit overwrought just now. Perhaps I do owe you an apology and a bit of an explanation. Maybe then you'll find me easier to accept, and that will be to the benefit of us both." A rustling sound emanated from the corner by the tallboy. "But first," he said, "be so good as to extinguish that light!"

Olivia's trembling hand obeyed.

"Let me reassure you," began Cyrus, "that I'm no happier about this situation than you are. It is much more to my liking to remain limbotic than to personify like this after so many years. As a matter of fact, it's downright discomfiting, so the sooner I can arrange to settle matters and desist, the happier I'll be. The speed with which that happens, Madam, depends in large part upon you."

"Surely this haunting has nothing to do with me!"

"Haunting!" Cyrus sneered. "What a naive concept." He rustled in irritation. "Haunting is the stuff of folk tales — a term used by the ill informed suggesting evil intent." He gave a snort. "Most of us delight in being rid of the bumblings of the corporeal world. If circumstances require us to manifest, we prefer to do it as inconspicuously as possible. Unfortunately, it depends in large measure on the luck of the bloody draw. And that, Madam, is where you come in."

"I'm afraid you're making very little sense to me," said Olivia. If this is madness, she thought, if I am witnessing the unraveling of my own mind, at least I'm right here in my bed, suffering no physical harm and causing no embarrassment to anybody else. Her curiosity overcame her better judgment.

"Please tell me, Great Great Grandfather Thornheart, how am I involved in all this?"

"Cyrus!" he bellowed, startling her with his vehemence. "You will address me as Cyrus. And I will call you Olivia for the duration of our association—may it bloody well be brief!"

"Cyrus," she giggled. Despite his bombastic delivery, he had a rather musical voice. She was beginning to enjoy herself.

"Very well, first things first. If you are to understand what I have to say, you must discard the myth of mortality to which your world subscribes. Death—or exanimation as we prefer to say—is not an ultimate, but rather a point on a continuum, a stage of the game, so to speak. In the same manner that one soul can be nearing death, another can be vivibund—on the verge of life. Believe me, one condition is just as unnerving as the other. In both cases, the pendulum can swing either way, depending on the combination of forces."

"What sort of forces?"

"Don't interrupt. You must realize that a spirit approaches manifestation in the corporeal world with the same degree of enthusiasm that a man faces death. Each prefers the status quo—for the man, immortality; for the spirit, evanescence. Neither, ultimately, has a choice. Are you with me so far, Olivia?"

"I'm not sure. You still haven't explained why you're here in my—this—bedroom or what it all has to do with me."

"Very well, then. You need to understand that the life choices one makes determine one's peace in the hereafter. Those who comport themselves humanely and maintain order in their affairs make the transition without pause. For others, an unresolved conflict or an unatoned sin delays evanescence until they settle the issue and earn the reward of nullity. As for me, neither controversy nor moral transgression brought me to this sorry state."

Cyrus paused, then began again in a gentler tone. "It was for love that I consigned myself to this infernal essence." His voice caught. "But if I were to live my life over, I'd bloody well do the same again!"

Olivia held her breath, waiting for him to continue. The silence swelled until it seemed larger than the room itself.

"At the final tally, a man has only his honor to separate him from lesser beings. So as a gentleman and a soldier, I gave my word—made a promise from the heart that neither hell nor the devil himself will prevent me from fulfilling. Yet, as I stated before, Olivia, your vulnerability—your acquiescence to the will of others—has been an impediment to my mission, a threat to my honor. I have squandered many years reviling you and railing against the injustice of my circumstances. But I have come to realize that you possess a man's intelligence, that you comprehend things other women can not. Like me, you value truth and are considered trustworthy by those whose lives you touch.

"When you first started speaking aloud in this empty house, I thought you were communing with the bloody cat, but later your questions clearly were directed to absent family members—your husband, your mother, your nephew Alexander. Little by little, I began to regard you less as a complication and more as a compatriot. Then finally tonight, before retiring, you addressed yourself to *me*, and I felt the time was right to risk your being receptive to my presence."

She thought she heard a shift of position, a slight click of heels.

"So here I stand, no longer regarding you as an obstacle, asking you if I may count on your assistance."

"Good grief!" said Olivia. "I can't imagine how!"

"Time," he answered quickly. "I need time to settle my unfinished business and make good my word." He took a deep breath. "But unless you agree to sustain me with your patronage, I will evanesce, and all will be lost."

"For heaven's sake!" cried Olivia. "Tell me what to do!"

His answer, when it came, was in a voice so weakened by weariness that it was barely audible. She leaned forward, straining to hear.

"Believe in me," he whispered.

hy, Miz Charlotte," exclaimed Lucy at the front door. "We haven't seen you for ages. Come on in, and I'll tell Miz Livvy y'all are here." She included Mary Finn with her smile and disappeared upstairs.

"What an incredible room!" said Mary Finn. Her professional eye overlooked the clutter of too much furniture and scrutinized the elaborate ceiling moldings, the four tall mullioned windows, and the parquet floor. A mantle of white marble graced the fireplace and matched the sills of the doors and windows. "I can see why you covet it."

"Don't you agree it'll make a wonderful inn?" Charlotte whispered. "I plan to have nine bedrooms—five upstairs, two on this floor if I convert the back parlor, and two downstairs on the kitchen level." Charlotte swept her hand in a proprietary manner. "I just know I can make it work if only I can pry Olivia out!"

"If I were your aunt, I'd die before I'd let it go. Look at this paneling!"

"Charlotte, dear." Olivia crossed the room with her

hands outstretched, and the two women touched cheeks. "What a nice surprise."

"Meet my friend, Mary Finn Hagin, Aunt Olivia. Mary Finn is in real estate."

"And what do you think of this old relic, Ms. Hagin?"

"It's charming," said Mary Finn. "Have you always lived here?"

"Oh, my, no. Hibiscus House belonged to the family of my husband, whom I knew from the time we were children. I moved here when we married."

"Such marvelous workmanship." Mary Finn caressed the inlaid wainscot. "Charlotte tells me there's a garden."

"Yes, with confederate jasmine and yellow lotus and Japanese iris just as it was originally planned in 1856. My housekeeper's son, Jonas, tends it for me. Would you care to see the upstairs?"

Charlotte and Mary Finn followed Olivia up the open staircase illumined by an oculus in the domed ceiling. A nine-foot-tall, mahogany four-poster dominated Olivia's bedroom where faded mauve and apple green blended in the harmony of another era. With two fingers' effort, Olivia lifted one of the floor-to-ceiling windows engineered to disappear into the attic and stepped out onto a balcony overlooking Forsyth Park.

"It's beautiful," said Mary Finn. "The man who built this house had elaborate tastes."

"Cyrus is — was — quite a formidable fellow. Much more of a romantic than one might think at first," said Olivia. "I'll show you his portrait on the way downstairs."

Behind the older woman's back, Charlotte shot a look at Mary Finn as the three of them continued their tour.

Two huge Savannah holly trees shaded the little table in

the garden where they had settled when Lucy arrived with the tea tray. Charlotte, ever carb conscious, declined the cinnamon cookies and passed them on to Mary Finn.

"Have you heard from Alexander?" asked Olivia, gathering Tomochichi into her lap.

"He sent Farley and me an anniversary gift last month — no note, just a small watercolor painting of a rather overblown Irish girl who Farley says looks 'ripe.' Like all of Alex's work, it uses colors oddly — greenish skin tones, that sort of thing. We hung it over the commode."

As disapproval flickered across Olivia's face, Mary Finn quickly redirected the conversation.

"Charlotte tells me Alexander lived with you before he moved abroad."

"Both my husband and his sister, Abigail Wade, died in 1975, and for about six months Charlotte and Alexander lived with their father and a housekeeper. But clearly they needed motherly nurturing, so the children came to live with me at Hibiscus House. Eventually, Charlotte married and made a home of her own. But Alexander, who is eight years younger, stayed with me until he grew up and went away to study art in Europe." The tenderness in her voice when she spoke of her nephew made her next words redundant.

"We were great pals," she said. "We spoke Pig Latin to each other and played chess — I never won — and watched old movies on television. I taught him to play the ukulele and he taught me — oh, so many things. When he first left, I thought my heart would break. He was the son I never had." She made a serious business of rearranging the cookies. "But he writes to me often, and I delight in his progress as a painter. I do believe one day he'll be recognized for his work. Just now he's learning about himself — building a portfolio of life experiences, you might say."

"He's thirty years old and has never had a real job in his life!" snapped Charlotte. "If Father hadn't left him a small trust, he'd be begging on the streets of Dublin. Farley offered him a position in his company — Alexander is, after all, good with his hands — but apparently the construction business isn't *aesthetic* enough for him. He'd rather live in a garret painting clouds than forgodsake do something useful with his talent." She squeezed her paper napkin into a damp ball.

"What are *you* doing these days, dear?" Olivia asked sweetly. Again Mary Finn sought a way to diffuse the situation.

"She's taken an interest in real estate. I'm afraid she might become very strong competition if I don't watch my step."

"By the way, Aunt Olivia, speaking of real estate," began Charlotte, "have you had this house appraised recently? You really should, you know, in case of fire."

"My lawyer, Charles Quinn, takes care of all that sort of thing for me. Carter had great faith in his judgment."

"Haven't you any curiosity about what it is worth?"

"The value of Hibiscus House to me can't be calculated in dollars and cents. Especially after meeting — especially now."

"The maintenance must be staggering. All these rooms for just one person to rattle around in alone."

"Not so alone," said Olivia absently. The two younger women exchanged puzzled glances.

"What do you mean — not so alone?" Charlotte leaned forward, intent on her aunt's face.

"An old house like this harbors any number of essences. Do you remember when you were a little girl we used to play 'if only walls could talk'? Well, I've learned recently if one is very quiet, one can plainly hear that indeed they sometimes do."

She's crazy as a loon, thought Charlotte. Listening to walls and speaking of the dead as if they are alive. "You should get out more," she said. "Play bridge, go shopping, have lunch with friends. It's not healthy to be so isolated."

Olivia chuckled, stroking the cat. "I'm not isolated. I often chat with people in the park and watch the children on the swings. Alice Maynard and her sister came to lunch just last Wednesday. And, of course, I have Lucy and Jonas."

"Have you given any thought to moving out of this place into something smaller, more manageable, where you would be among other people your age?" The edge to Charlotte's voice matched her profile, her fingernails, her shins.

"If you mean a retirement community, good gracious no! But I have thought of traveling a bit. I've never seen the Grand Canyon, for one. And of course there's Alexander over in Ireland. Lucy and Jonas would look after the house for me—perhaps even move in while I'm away. It would please me to think of them spending Christmas at Hibiscus House. If ever there were anyone deserving of happiness, it's Lucy. She's been my dearest friend."

Charlotte could barely contain her exasperation. "Aunt Olivia, you needn't go to such lengths. Farley and I will be delighted to oversee your affairs if you go away."

As if in response, Tomochichi shot up from Olivia's lap and pounced stiff-legged into the center of the table looking for all the world as if his tail had been plugged into a 220-volt socket. For a moment he hissed and batted furiously at the air, scattering cookies and overturning Charlotte's teacup into her lap, then catapulted into the holly tree and scrabbled over the fence.

"My skirt!" wailed Charlotte, mopping vigorously. "What's the matter with that animal?"

"Something just spooked him," soothed Mary Finn, handing Charlotte her napkin and restoring order to the tabletop. "Cats are like that sometimes."

"Spooked?" A tiny chime of amusement rang in Olivia's voice. "Yes, perhaps he was at that."

G ood morning," trilled the receptionist. "Welcome to Three Palms. How may I help you?"

"I'm here to make inquiries about your facility on behalf of my aunt," said Charlotte. She noted the tasteful art work on the paneled walls, the vase of fresh flowers on a glass table, the inviting leather sofa and chairs.

"Then you need to speak with Mr. Vick, who should be here any minute. Perhaps you'd care to have a seat?"

Charlotte squinted at the woman's name tag. "Well, Madge, can you just tell me if you have room for new, uh, residents?" She had almost said "cases" but caught herself just in time.

"Mr. Vick will be happy to answer all your questions. Would you like a cup of coffee while you wait?"

"Is there at least a brochure I could look at?"

Madge plucked one from her top drawer and handed it to Charlotte, who settled on a chair across the room. "Forty-two comfortably elegant suites," she read. "On-site nursing care. Housekeeping and laundry services. All meals." This, thought Charlotte, is going to be the best possible place to park Olivia. The remoteness of Three Palms' "beautiful, two-acre campus" located "a mile off highway 17 in South Carolina" suited Charlotte perfectly. Not only would lack of public transportation solve the Lucy problem, but more importantly, it would keep Olivia from interfering with the remodeling of Hibiscus House.

A tall man with a drooping moustache pushed through the glass doors and hurried across to Madge's desk. "Did Doctor Lindsey return my call?" he asked.

"No sir, not yet. But you have a visitor." She indicated Charlotte.

"Sorry you had to wait," the man said, offering his hand. "I'm Donald Vick, director of Three Palms."

"Charlotte Horner. I've come here on behalf of my aunt."

"I see." He smiled. "Would you like to have a little tour?"

"That's not really necessary. I've learned from your brochure all I need to know, except, of course, about availability."

"We currently have two openings. I could show you one of our suites if you wish."

"How soon could my aunt move in?"

Mr. Vick hesitated. "Forgive me, Ms. Horner, if I seem, uh, surprised. Checking out the suites is usually the first thing families of prospective residents want to do. It's very important to reassure themselves that their loved ones will be well cared for in pleasant surroundings."

"I'm a bit short on time," said Charlotte. "Perhaps another day. How soon?"

"Both available suites are being repainted at present.

I'm estimating it will be a couple of weeks until either one will be available for showing. Is your aunt in good health?"

"She's physically able," said Charlotte. "But she's . . . slipping a bit mentally, I'm afraid. To the point that we worry about her judgment, if you get my drift."

Mr. Vick smiled. "Our staff is well equipped to handle such situations. I'm sure Three Palms can accommodate her needs. Perhaps the next step — once the suites are ready for viewing — would be to set up an appointment so your aunt can see what we have to offer. Then, if she's amenable, the three of us can sit down and discuss financial arrangements. In the meantime, here is my card. And I hope you won't mind filling out a preliminary form so we can be in touch."

Ten minutes later, Charlotte headed for her car, her spirits buoyant. What luck to score on the first try. She had imagined weeks of going from one depressing place to the next, each smelling of urine and bad food and, well, old people. But Three Palms wasn't like that. It had a swimming pool, forgodsakes, and a beauty salon — more like a resort than the geriatric holding tank she had anticipated. One day Aunt Olivia would thank her for the chance to relocate to such pleasant surroundings. Yesssssss! she thought with a grin.

She liked the clicking sound her high heels made on the cement walkway — and for one wild moment she felt like skipping. Get a grip, Charlotte, she cautioned herself. Hibiscus House isn't yours yet.

As she approached her car while rummaging in her purse for her keys, the toe of her sandal caught, causing Charlotte to fall hard on one knee, wrenching her shoulder, and banging her forehead against the driver's side door. Her purse went flying, strewing its contents in the process.

"Christ!" she swore, as she pulled herself into a sitting position and began to assess the damage. Blood already seeped through a tear in the knee of her new silk slacks. She inspected the pavement to see what had caused her to trip, but for the life of her she could see no irregularities, no impediments, no reason whatsoever for her fall.

"Let me give you a hand," said Mr. Vick, taking her elbow. "I happened to glance out the window just as you went down. Are you okay?" He helped her to stand, then bent to gather up the contents of her purse.

Charlotte's face flamed with embarrassment as he retrieved the silver flask and returned it to the purse without comment. "I think so, but my leg is bleeding."

Vick handed her the purse, then leaned closer to inspect the goose egg rising on her forehead. "Nancy Willis, our staff nurse, is on duty," he said. "Let's get you back inside and have her take a look at you."

* * *

At a quarter past one, Charlotte drove up and over the Talmadge Bridge, her left knee bandaged and throbbing, her mood as black as her newly ruined slacks. She hated the thought of going to lunch in torn, bloody clothing, but Mary Finn hadn't answered her cell phone, and Charlotte was already fifteen minutes late for their date. No time to go home and change. She glanced at her face in the rear view mirror. Maybe with artful rearranging, her hair could hide the knot purpling on her forehead.

Normally, she enjoyed lunching at Toucan Café with its bright colors and excellent menu. The cheery atmosphere encouraged a lively lunch crowd, and she nearly always ran into someone she knew. But at the moment, all she wanted to do was go home, take a couple of aspirin, and lie down. She locked her car and limped across the parking lot, watching carefully where she stepped.

"Good God," said Mary Finn as Charlotte approached the table. "You look like you've been mugged! What happened?"

"Why in hell do you even *have* a cell phone if you aren't going to answer it?" Charlotte snapped. "Order me a grilled Portobello and a glass of Chablis. I'm going to the ladies." She limped across the room and disappeared around the corner.

When their orders came, Mary Finn waited patiently, letting her soup grow cold rather than irritate Charlotte further by starting to eat without her. Charlotte, in an evil mood, was prone to bitching at the wait staff, and Mary Finn didn't wish to be embarrassed. But when her difficult friend still had not returned after twenty minutes, Mary Finn rose to investigate. Not until she crossed the empty side room and reached the little back hall where the restrooms were located did she hear the racket—a rhythmic pounding punctuated by a wail. "Why-y-y won't someone hel-l-lp!" Bang. Bang, Bang.

"Charlotte, is that you?" called Mary Finn.

"Forgodsake, get me out of here!" yelled Charlotte. "I can't unlock the door!"

"Hang on," called Mary Finn. "I'll go get help."

By this time, a few curious onlookers had gathered at the end of the short hall. "What's wrong in there?" a woman asked, her eyes wide with concern. "Is someone sick?"

Mary Finn grabbed the arm of a passing waitress. "Get someone to come immediately and open the ladies' room door," she hissed. "It's stuck, and my friend can't get out." The girl nodded and hurried away.

"They're coming," Mary Finn reassured Charlotte. "Just stay calm. They're going to get you out."

"Fuck, fuck, *fuck!*" screeched Charlotte on the other side of the closed door. "I broke the heel of my sandal banging on the goddamn door. Why did you wait so long?"

When not a single key on his chain would release the lock, the manager called for backup, dispatching one waiter to fetch a hammer and chisel and another to keep onlookers from getting in the way. "Please step back, folks," he said. "We need to remove this door." Tools in hand, he began chipping away at layers of old paint and pounding out the hinge pins, the thwack of each blow doubled by the echoing hallway. It seemed to take forever, but at last the heavy door came free, releasing Charlotte who emerged, sweating and furious.

"You can expect a call from my lawyer," she snarled at her rescuer. "And you can also eat the cost of my lunch. I'm out of here." Without another word to anyone, she limped across the waiting area and pushed through the door into the searing afternoon heat. Thunderclouds had gathered, mirroring her mood.

Charlotte pressed her fingers against her temples as waves of pain spiked across the top of her head. "It's like I'm being forgodsake punished," she muttered, picking her way across the parking lot in her damaged shoe. She felt justifiably sulky and pissed — at Mary Finn for not coming to her aid sooner, at the unctuous apologies of that bozo manager, at having ruined her Cole Haan sandals and her new Armani slacks, and most of all at Aunt Olivia for being such a useless, irritating, old-fool impediment to her plans.

Just as she felt the first drop of rain, the window of her car suddenly exploded outward, spewing glass fragments in all directions. She stood frozen in shock, numbly aware of having narrowly escaped serious injury. Now, because she had ignored Farley's caution always to leave a crack open on a very hot day, she had no driver's side window. With a thunderstorm about to happen! What else could possibly go wrong?

Ten minutes before she reached the shelter of her garage, the heavens opened, driving torrents in through the open window and drenching her hair, her clothes, and the expensive leather upholstery upon which she had insisted. "I don't deserve this!" Charlotte railed. "What did I forgodsake do?"

*T*he crash so startled Jonas Bates that he almost swallowed his mouthful of ten-penny nails. What in hell had the kid done now? He shook his head. The boss shoulda canned Danny two months ago — the *first* time he screwed up instead of the fiftieth. Kid seem like he tryin' for some kind of record! Jonas thought. He jammed his hammer through the loop of his overalls and walked down the hall to investigate.

When he stepped into the future master bedroom, his mouth dropped open. A 30-gallon drum of tile adhesive lay lidless on its side pumping its sticky, black contents all over the newly sanded hardwood flooring. From the look of its bashed-in side, it had either been struck hard with a heavy object or dropped from a significant height. But there was nowhere from which it could have fallen and no such implement in sight. Except for the drum and a couple of saw horses, the room was empty.

"Danny!" he roared. But it was Henry who came on the run.

"He's gone, Jonas," he said, mopping his forehead on his grimy sleeve.

"Where to?"

"I dunno. He was out back loading trash into Sam's pickup when all of a sudden he come flying around the side of the house with his eyes buggin' out and took off on that old bike of his."

"Who was back there with him?"

"Nobody." Henry stuck his hands in his pockets and rocked back on his heels. "Sam was working with me in the kitchen, and Alf's gone to pick up supplies. Far as I know, he was by hisself."

Jonas cast his palms at the ceiling. "Well, what do you think pissed him off?"

"He didn't seem pissed, Jonas—he seemed scared to death. Acted like he was running from something he couldn't get away from fast enough. What the hell happened here?" He bent to inspect the overturned drum.

"That's what I'd like to know," said Jonas. "Go call the office and have 'em send somebody over to clean up this mess." He pulled a red bandanna from his hip pocket and blew his nose.

Goddamn restoration business, he thought as he walked back down the hall. Always something going wrong. If it wasn't bad plumbing or leaking roofs, it was termites in the walls and crumbling foundations. Nothing was ever square, ever plumb, ever goddamn easy!

He grabbed a handful of nails and bent over to toenail a stud. But as he started to swing, the nail seemed to shift slightly to the right. Irritated, he repositioned it, holding it firmly at the base. This time as he raised his hammer, the nail shifted slightly to the left.

My goddamn eyes are going, he thought, rubbing them hard with both index fingers. Then he wiped his glasses on the bandanna and repositioned them on his nose. The third time, he set the nail with a couple of light taps, then swung smartly, bringing the hammer down hard on his left thumb with a blow that sent him Indian dancing around the room.

"God*damn!*" he yelled as the pain shot up his arm. His thumbnail immediately started to turn black. He'd lose it for sure.

As he sat on the sawhorse shaking his injured hand and inspecting the damage, one of its legs collapsed, and he crashed over backwards, sending his glasses flying and lacerating his right palm on the blade of a hacksaw.

"God*damn!*" he shouted again. The room swirled as a slow motion galaxy exploded in his head. Henry, taking the stairs two at a time, hurried to his friend's side and peered down into his face.

"Jeez, Jonas, you okay?"

With his right hand Jonas examined his forehead, leaving a smear of blood in its place.

"Before we even started this job, I told my mama I had a real bad feeling about it. Never should have signed on in the first place." He spoke through chattering teeth, for a sudden chill had gripped him, and his whole body trembled convulsively. "Oh, man, I got to go home," he said. Rolling onto his knees, he half-crawled to the door and hauled himself to his feet with the doorknob. He waited for the spinning room to steady, then gathered up the pieces of his broken glasses and staggered into the hall.

"That goddamn kid better have his ass back on the job by eight o'clock tomorrow morning or he's history," he muttered. He waived away Henry's offer of help and hobbled toward the stairs.

Halfway down, a rotten board gave way beneath his weight with a loud crack. "I-i-i-i-e-e-e!" Jonas sang as his left foot made a xylophone of the spindled banister and the nails in his apron sprayed like shrapnel. From the top of the staircase, Henry watched his buddy cartwheel to the bottom, plunge head first into a stack of two-by-fours, and knock himself out cold.

Navigating the stairs as quickly as he could, Henry knelt beside Jonas, breathing hard, unsure about what to do. Gingerly, he lifted first one eyelid, then the other. He placed an ear to his friend's chest, listening for his heart.

"You just lay there," he said, "and don't try to move nothing. I'm going to get Sam." As he hurried toward the back of the house, a sound caused him to pause, and turn, and freeze in place. Beyond Jonas Bates' crumpled form, the open front door scraped across the planked flooring and swung shut with a metallic click.

* * *

"What's all that noise?" Olivia shouted into the telephone. "Who's crying?"

"Just somebody's sick chile," yelled Lucy. "Me and Henry are at Memorial Hospital."

"Henry who?"

"I don't rightly know — some workman who called the ambulance to carry Jonas to the emergency room after he fell down the stairs at work. Then he come round to fetch me in his truck. Henry, I mean, not Jonas. Hold your horses, mister. I'll be done with this phone in just a minute."

"Lucy, is Jonas seriously hurt?"

"His hand is all cut up, and his glasses is broke, and he hit his head hard enough to knock hisself out. They won't know whether any bones is fractured 'til after they finished with the X-rays. Henry thinks he gonna need some stitches — Jonas I mean, not Henry. Anyway, I wanted you to know where I am in case you need me 'cause of course Sis don't never answer the phone. Okay, mister, don't get yer dangle in a tangle. I'm hangin' up. Got to go, Miz Livvy, or this here feller's gonna wet hisself right here in the hall."

"Will you please call me when you get home? I'll be so worried."

"Now don't you go frettin' about Jonas. He got a hard old head — just like his daddy. But I'll call you just the same."

*T*omo-chee-che-e-e!" called Olivia. "Where *is* that cat?" For two weeks he had been behaving peculiarly. Usually lethargic, he had taken to popping unexpectedly out of closets, making weird sounds, and disappearing for days at a time. He even *looked* strange, all fluffed up and militant, brandishing his tail like a bayonet. She supposed it was spring calling forth some remnant of masculinity long ago sacrificed on the altar of veterinary science.

Perched on the corner of the chimney, the full moon washed the garden in silver while a breeze, rich with the perfume of new greenery, brought a tang of salt from the ocean. Olivia breathed deeply of its fragrance, savoring the stillness.

On just such a night as this, she had danced with Carter at Tybrisa Pavilion out at the end of the long fishing pier. She remembered the warmth of his hand at her back, the sweet, soapy smell of his cheek. An hour earlier she had stood before her parent's boudoir window watching for the Thornheart's silver-grey Packard to turn into the drive and thinking over her mother's words: "A proper courtship," Elizabeth Gaylord had instructed, "requires the gentleman to be punctual, displaying honor and reliability, and the lady to be reticent, suggesting she has other options." Eager as Olivia was, she knew that making Carter wait fifteen minutes would be mandatory lest she violate her mother's standards of good taste.

At precisely eight o'clock, she ducked behind the drape as headlights swept the front of the house. In the dark she watched Carter emerge from the car, tug at his cuffs, and disappear beneath the roof of the porte couchère.

Below she could hear her father's questioning bass, Carter's baritone, her mother's gentle soprano. A perfunctory glance at her reflection confirmed what she already knew — that lovely hair and a flattering neckline could not compensate for a rather broad mouth and freckles. Yet even she had to admit her high color improved her face. Could it be that Carter saw in her something she did not?

At ten minutes after eight, she could pace no longer. She touched an extra dab of Chanel No. 5 at the base of her throat, draped her stole over her arm and, marshalling a tiny army of defiance, marched to the living room.

Olivia swayed in the moonlight, remembering how well they had danced together. Over his shoulder a blur of smiling faces spun like a slow carousel, and she, lightheaded from Carter's fresh-scrubbed fragrance, wondered if she would ever be quite so happy again. I will always remember this night, she vowed. And so she had.

She shot the burglar bolt on the back door and, pausing to switch off a lamp here, to straighten a pillow there, made her way upstairs.

Poor Charlotte, she thought as she turned down her

bed covers. For someone with all the accouterments of comfort, she certainly seemed dissatisfied, as if her life, like an unbalanced diet, had given her an acid tongue. Perhaps if she and Farley had a child . . . But it was unlikely that at almost thirty-nine Charlotte would suddenly decide to start a family. And given her nature, that was certainly for the best.

Olivia pulled on her nightgown and began plucking pins from her hair. That left the future of the family to Alexander, who thus far showed little inclination toward fatherhood. She could visualize his restless hands mixing colors on a palette, but the image of them cradling a baby would not take shape. Darling Alexander. How lonely he had sounded in the letter she received in the afternoon mail. She fetched it from her little writing desk and reread it in the light of her bedside lamp, her glasses perched on the tip of her nose.

March 23, 2004
Dublin, Ireland

Dearest Auntie O.,

I have set the kettle on to boil for my third cup of morning tea and am sitting here counting chimney pots across the rooftops of the Coombe. There are hundreds of them in this dreary section of the city, and most are spewing smoke into the already gray day as if purging evil spirits from the rowhouses below. In a moment I'll top off my mug with Irish whiskey in an attempt to warm my freezing fingers and purge my own evil spirits. Maybe then I can focus on the task at hand — sketches for a small mural I have been commissioned to do — and stop dwelling on loneliness and all that's rotten in the world.

My mood is partly due to this damned climate — crypt-cold and raw — and to knowing that your dogwood tree is in full bloom on the other side of the ocean. But mostly it is because of nagging self-doubts. Does my work speak my mind? Am I capable of producing art that will endure? Or am I merely a facile craftsman churning out calendar crap for the masses to be discarded with the Christmas wreath every December 31st?

I keep reminding myself how fortunate I am compared to others who wrestle with similar demons. Thanks to Father and to you, I have both financial and emotional support. Knowing that my room in Hibiscus House is there — should I decide to chuck it all and come home — both comforts me and strengthens my resolve.

I remember, too, what you told me that winter we spent building the Abigail Ann: "If a thing is worth doing, it's worth doing right — and that takes work." The little schooner sits on my book shelf urging me back to my easel.

The steam is up, so I'll close now and post this in the afternoon. Sorry about all the doom and gloom. But after all (I hear you say), that's what pals are for.

Take care of yourself, and give Lucy a hug for me.

All my love,

Alexander

She tucked the letter into its envelope and pulled the quilt to her chin. Young people are bound to feel insecure about themselves at times, she thought, especially those as sensitive as Alexander. His self-doubts will disappear once he's chalked up a few successes.

His loneliness, however, was something else altogether. She wished she could be there to wrap her arms around him. As a matter of fact, she could do with a hug herself. Olivia swallowed hard. First thing in the morning she would write a nice, long letter full of encouragement and happy news. Like what? That she was hearing voices that other people didn't? That she feared Charlotte was trying to pressure her into moving out of Hibiscus House? Happy news seemed to be in short supply these days. Even Tomochichi was acting deranged!

She snapped off her bedside lamp and closed her eyes with a sigh, vaguely aware of something odd, missing, left undone. On the verge of sleep she remembered what it was.

"Why didn't Lucy call?" she asked aloud.

"Because she has other issues on her mind," said Cyrus. "Have you reached a decision?" He rustled noisily in the dark.

"About what?" asked Olivia, startled. "Oh, I do wish you wouldn't pounce like that!"

"About whether or not I may count on your support. It makes a difference as to how I proceed."

"If by 'support' you mean will I proclaim myself a true believer in ghosts, I'm afraid not. The best I can do, Cyrus, is promise to remain open-minded. Have you been bedeviling my cat?"

He chuckled. "Bloody little beast. How was I to know he'd react like that? I apologize for disrupting your little garden party the other day, Olivia, although that impertinent young woman certainly deserved a lapful of tea. I'm still a bit awkward, I guess. Today was even worse."

"In what way?"

"I had a sentimental urge to visit Major William

Goode's house on Bolton Street where I lived for the first two years of my marriage. Its rooms were quite comfortable, though not nearly so grand as these. I especially liked the master bedroom on the second floor with its rounded turret window where one could look out over the lawns and watch the carriages go by."

"I know which house you mean," she said. It once belonged to my friend Hattie Bodean before it was broken up into apartments. The new owners are remodeling it into condominiums—one on each floor—so of course all the tenants were given notice to vacate. One of them was Jonas Bates, my housekeeper's son. But you're right. It could still be a lovely house if only it were properly maintained."

Cyrus sighed. "I almost wish I hadn't returned. Now two other houses occupy the green where the ladies gathered to play that new French game croquet. They've ruined William's house, Olivia, stripped it of its warm woods and soft colors. The fireplace is closed, and new walls are being erected willy nilly into little boxes. What an awful jumble the world has become."

His words seemed to summon a sudden chill to the room, and Olivia snugged the quilt up under her chin. "*Tempus edax rerum*, as Papa used to say. Time changes all things."

A wicked little chuckle rattled out of the darkness. "Well, maybe eventually, but not just yet."

"Oh, dear, I'm afraid to ask."

"No cause to worry," he assured her. "I merely discommoded the craftsmen a bit—if one can call them craftsmen."

"How did you do that?"

"I've found that dull-witted people are often highly

sensitive to auras and essences. Unfortunately, they become frightened when they can't comprehend what they sense. One such limited chap persisted in trashing some oak window casements ripped from William Goode's day parlor." He chuckled again. "When I dissuaded him from doing so, he elected to depart — rather abruptly, ha!"

Was that a little dance step Olivia heard over in the corner by the radiator? "What kind of 'dissuasion'?" she asked warily.

"Harmless, my dear — a whispered word in his ear, a bit of icy tingle down the back of his trousers. Anyway, I decided to test on one of the other chaps the theory that with minimal manifestation, I might be able to influence the direction of small events — rather like a wind shift that can alter the course of a sailing ship. However, my clumsy efforts sent him tumbling down the stairs instead. I'm beginning to realize that 'haunting' (as you say) like any other art requires practice."

Olivia gasped. "So it was *you!* Cyrus Morton Thornheart, do you realize that your little prank nearly killed Lucy's son, Jonas? At the very least it sent him to the hospital with I don't know *what* kind of injuries! You should be ashamed of yourself for behaving like a spoiled, wicked, ill-mannered, self-indulgent . . ."

"I say, woman! Be silent and give a man a chance."

"And not one whit of remorse!" Olivia smacked her pillow for emphasis.

"On the contrary," said Cyrus in a voice softened by contrition. "I am heartily sorry my ineptitude brought harm to the lad, although I assure you, he'll be none the worse for it in a day or two." He humphed and harrumphed for a minute or two, shuffling his feet first near the window, then over by the fireplace. Olivia, reminded of past confrontations with Charlotte's willful behavior, said nothing and let him stew.

"If it will appease you," he said finally. "I'll try do something to make amends."

Her mind suddenly flew off in all directions, imagining the results of Cyrus' bumbling efforts to atone—erupting beer steins, bursting basketballs, dollar-spewing ATMs . . . "I think you've done quite enough already," said Olivia, stifling a tiny giggle that threatened to bubble up from the base of her throat.

"Nonsense," he snapped. "I've only just begun. There's a reason for my practicing, Olivia. I'm on a mission, as I've already explained, and the sooner I can accomplish it, the better off we'll all be."

"You must promise not to make any more mischief for Lucy's family. She is my dearest friend, and she has enough on her mind without your devilment."

"I do make you that promise," he said solemnly, "and you know what lengths I'll go to keep it."

"Then on whom do you plan to 'practice' next?"

"I'd rather not say, but rest assured the person in question got a sampling of my increasing skill this afternoon. The explosion was my masterpiece." A chortle rattled out of the darkness.

"Explosion? What explosion? Was anybody injured?"

"Just the littlest bit," he admitted. "Mostly to her dignity. A necessary part of the plan, Olivia. Sometimes one must get the attention of those who refuse to cooperate before they can be humbled into compliance. My hope is that the punishment meted out today to the tart in question will bring her into line. Let's leave it at that."

* * *

Olivia punched her pillow savagely, furious with herself for falling asleep in the middle of her conversation with Cyrus. He had been talking about meting out punishment, and now she couldn't be sure where his words ended and her dreams began. She lay contemplating a watery shimmer on the wall — morning sunshine reflecting from a puddle of yesterday's rain on the piazza outside her window.

Real as it had seemed, she was sure she had dreamed the part about standing beside Cyrus while talking with Charlotte on the telephone. It had been a particularly disturbing call, but try as she might she could not remember Charlotte's words — only the agitation they produced. Nor could she recall how Cyrus looked, although she had seen him clearly. Had he warned her against Charlotte, or had that been part of the dream too? Perhaps their entire conversation was conjured up in sleep. Maybe her age was catching up with her, loosening her grip on reality, and Cyrus himself was merely a figment of her imagination.

Olivia smiled to herself. She had to admit that, even if she had dreamed Cyrus up, she thoroughly enjoyed the delusion. She had developed a real fondness for him, egotistical and difficult though he might be, and could sense, by his rustlings, the changes in his mood. He amused her with his blustering and flattered her with his trust. Yes, she genuinely liked the crusty old spook and looked forward to his visits.

Olivia heard the back door shut and Lucy's steps descend to the kitchen. She hurried out of bed and into her robe and slippers, reminding herself that what little information she had on Jonas' condition had *not* come from a reliable source. The aroma of coffee greeted her as she descended the staircase.

"Mornin', Miz Livvy," said Lucy, bending over to pour cat chow into a plastic saucer. "I woulda called you last night, but me and Henry didn't leave the hospital till after 9 p.m."

"That's all right, Lucy dear. But tell me, how is Jonas?"

"He moaning and groaning 'cause he got a goose egg on his head, a few stitches in one hand, and some stiffness in his joints — in other words, about as much hurtin' as you and me got on a daily basis." She slapped her thigh and cackled at Olivia. "He be fine in a day or two."

"So I heard."

"What?"

"I mean, so I figured — when you didn't call." Olivia poured two cups of coffee and handed Lucy hers, then settled at the kitchen table to share the hour of the morning both enjoyed the most.

Lucy sighed. "Like rushin' to the hospital yesterday wasn't bad enough. Like I didn't walk in the door to find Sis complaining about nobody cookin' her supper." She fished an envelope from her straw tote and handed it to Olivia. "This here's another thing that greeted me when I got home last night."

Unfolding the single sheet, Olivia read:

NOTICE TO TENANTS

As of April 1, 2004, the owners have listed for sale the property at 315 Hall Street, Savannah, Georgia 31401. Tenants are requested to make said property available for showing by appointment,

IN ACCORDANCE WITH THEIR LEASE AGREEMENT. PLEASE
DIRECT INQUIRIES TO THIS OFFICE.

FRANKLIN & HAY REALTY

Aghast, Olivia searched her friend's face. "Oh my
goodness, what shall we do?"

"That's what I keep asking myself," Lucy said, spooning
sugar into her coffee. "Me and Aunt Sis and Jonas—the
whole time he was comin' up—lived in that old house so
long I guess we come to think of it as ours. Now they go and
stick a big old ugly 'for sale' sign right in the middle of my
front yard." She slammed her cup down so hard it nearly
shattered. "When somebody buys our house, we gonna have
to move, and with rents risin' up so high in this part of town,
it'll have to be over to Pooler or Rincon or somewhere way
out south. I tell you, Miz Livvy, sometimes I think marrying
Mr. Bates was the biggest mistake I ever made!"

Accustomed to Lucy's non-sequiturs, Olivia knew if she
waited long enough, the muddy waters would clear.

"We gonna live the good life, he always say. We gonna
work hard and save money and get us a piece of land where
we can grow onions. He always readin' about soil and
fertilizer like the next day he gonna start planting. Year after
year we don't even save enough money to get us our own
house—let alone a onion farm! Now he's in his grave, rest
his soul, and not only do I got to see to myself and Jonas—I
got to take care of Mr. Bates' *sister* for the rest of her natural
life!"

Lucy got up and slammed a piece of bread into the
toaster. "Onions!" she muttered in disgust.

With years of practice, Olivia deftly rerouted Lucy's train of thought.

"You once told me Mr. Bates liked to sing."

"He liked makin' all kinds of music. Never had no lessons, but he could play the church organ like a dream— big, swelling sounds that made my breath come short." She settled opposite Olivia again and began to butter toast. "Always making music," she said with a twinkle. "If he didn't have nothing else, he'd pick up a couple of spoons and make 'em pop and rattle like they was alive. And hambone? That man could hambone better'n God." She sighed.

"I remember how he taught Alexander to do it," laughed Olivia. "Those two! What a pair they made."

"One time his boss told him to clean out an old house in Thunderbolt they was about to tear down. So Mr. Bates and his brother Ben spent all day loading broken tables and old window screens and such into the back of Ben's open truck. Nothing they found was worth keeping 'cept a old upright piano with some missing keys. Him and his brother loaded that piano in the truck last thing, and off they go down through Thunderbolt with Ben at the wheel and Mr. Bates sitting in the back at that piano just playin' and singin' and stompin' his foot like the circus come to town! Folks started following—kids and dogs and ladies waving aprons—until they was a regular parade going down River Drive. You never saw such a sight!" Lucy wiped her eyes. "Oh, he was a rare one, Mr. Bates. God, how I loved that man!"

She quickly shoved away from the table and began rattling dishes at the sink. The cuckoo clock on the wall struck nine, buying her some time.

"Anyway," said Lucy matter-of-factly, "don't none of that matter no more. One day after Mr. Bates passed on, I called up the Salvation Army and told 'em to come haul that old piano away. Just like *that* it was gone. I can't be bothered with all that foolishness." She gave her dishtowel a savage snap and went off to answer the telephone.

She returned a moment later, her expression grim. "I got to go. That was Jonas. He say Aunt Sis havin' chest pains and he can't drive her to the hospital 'cause his car is still over at the job. So I got to go take her in a cab." She untied her apron and hung it on the pantry doorknob. "I swear, if it ain't one thing." She grabbed her straw tote and marched like Sherman out the back door.

ith careful jockeying, Alexander was able to fit all twelve canvases into the back seat of his Morris Mini. He covered them with an old blanket and went back inside for his wallet and the envelope bearing Liam Thane's address. With luck the old girl would make the trip to Killiney and back without succumbing to whatever ailment caused white exhaust to plume from her tailpipe. He had even less knowledge about automobiles than he had interest in them, regarding them as a necessary, occasionally irritating fact of life. It didn't occur to him that he could afford a newer, more dependable vehicle — perhaps one with an automatic transmission to relieve him of the awkward business of shifting gears. Though dexterous, Alexander drove badly, so distracted was he by the passing scene.

Today, for the first time in months, the raw chill was missing from the air, and a thin sunshine held promise that spring was on the way. He turned up the collar of his army surplus jacket and rolled down his window to catch a whiff of the Irish Sea as he turned onto the Coast Road. A pang of homesickness caught him by surprise, and for a moment he wished this were the road to Tybee Island beach back home in Savannah.

Until his seventh Christmas when he discovered the magic of poster paint, sand had been Alexander's medium. Its whimsy delighted him — hot and powdery between his bare toes one moment, cool and malleable the next. On its smooth face he had scrawled messages to be collected and delivered by the surf. Once, transfixed by his perfect footprints, he had walked backward for a half mile down the shoreline before a lifeguard in a dune buggy plucked him up and returned him to the shade of Aunt Olivia's beach umbrella.

Consistency was the challenge — the adding of just enough sea water to make sand hold its shape. Too much and it sagged into a formless heap. A citadel with crenellated towers and a driftwood drawbridge rose at his royal bidding. Under his command whole battlefields revealed themselves, replete with bunkers and trenches. On his knees he probed the mystery of moon craters that flooded of their own accord. With each receding tide, new treasures surfaced — iridescent shells, the elbows of old trees — as if like Pompeii a whole civilization lay awaiting discovery if only he knew where to dig.

Alexander's rumbling stomach reminded him that he had forgotten lunch. He checked his watch to see if he had time to stop at the King's Rook for a pint and a sandwich. Good, he thought. Nearly an hour before my appointment with Liam Thane. He wiped his palms on his jeans. Is everyone this nervous about going public with his work? he wondered. Do poets feel the same tremulous, slightly nauseating constriction in the solar plexis when others read their words? The front wheel spun onto the gravel berm snapping his attention back to the moment. How easy it would be to yank the steering wheel to the left and launch himself and his paintings into Killiney Bay.

Instead he coaxed the Mini up to 60 m.p.h., exchanging waves with a busload of tourists debarking for a look at Bullock Castle.

Soon after rounding Sorrento Point, he braced himself for the view — an unimpeded vista from Dalkey Island to Bray Head. And in between, azure and calm, the bay blended hazily with the sky. Its beauty soothed him, and he released his anxiety to the salt air. What did the locals say? "See Killiney Bay and die."

Cobalt, thought Alex, feeling his spirits rise. Fading to cerulean at the horizon. Generally he was impatient with seascapes, preferring the challenge of the human form: the balance of the skeleton, the tension of muscles, the shadow play of light upon the planes of the face. But color fed his visual appetite, and he analyzed the hues of his environment as automatically as a master chef deciphers the flavors of herbs and spices.

Behind, the blast of a horn brought him upright; a red roadster, top down, followed in his wake. Unable to pass on the curving highway, the driver drummed impatiently on the steering wheel while his passenger held on to a broad-brimmed straw hat with a ribbon fluttering out behind.

They must be freezing, thought Alex. He looked helplessly for a safe place to pull over and allow them to pass. But the road wound narrowly around the cliff, and the Mini, already laboring on the incline, had no choice but to remain squarely in the convertible's path. He heaved a sigh of relief when, at the first opportunity, the red car shot around him as the driver hoisted his middle finger in a rude salute.

The small unpleasantness was enough to shatter Alexander's fragile optimism, and self-doubt once more began to fray him at the edges.

Will Liam Thane find my work amateurish? Are twelve canvases too many? Too few? Was it a mistake to have included the "Kirk of Corey?" He ran his fingertips across his chin and considered, for the first time, his own appearance. He knew he needed a haircut, but at least his hair was clean. Perhaps he shouldn't have worn jeans and a turtle-neck sweater; somewhere in his closet was the dark blue suit he had worn to Charlotte's wedding. My God, that was over a decade ago. It must be hopelessly out of style.

Five minutes later he pulled into the King's Rook car park and locked the Mini. Someone had propped open the pub door with a wooden keg in which wan geraniums struggled for life. He savored the dank aroma of ale and welcomed the interior gloom like a Neanderthal returning to the safety of his cave.

"Guinness," said Alex to the girl behind the bar. "And a sandwich — whatever you've got."

"That'll be €6.75," she said, sliding a pint across the bar.

He paid her, then pulled off his jacket and started to fling it over the next stool. But it was occupied by a straw hat with a long, green ribbon. He noticed that a glass half filled with tonic sat primly on a napkin — and next to it a pair of oversized sunglasses.

He recognized her immediately as she emerged from the ladies' loo and slipped into place, smoothing her corduroy skirt beneath her. She seemed to be alone.

"Hello again," he smiled.

"Have we met?" Wide-set eyes appraised him coolly. Were they green?

"Not formally, although your boyfriend did nearly nudge my old Morris off the cliff awhile ago. He must have been mighty thirsty." He hoped his smile softened his tone.

"I apologize for Derek," she said solemnly. "I always seem to be apologizing for Derek. He's really rather nice when you get to know him." She glanced at him sideways. "Being obnoxious is his tragic flaw." She grinned, and something brittle inside Alex turned rubbery.

"However, he's not my boyfriend," she added. "Derek is my brother."

She nodded toward a dark corner where he sat in earnest conversation with a pretty girl with upswept hair. "He was late for a rendezvous."

"Nice car," said Alex.

"Yes, a Porsche suits him."

"You're not Irish."

"No, Isle of Wight. Cowes, actually. I'm on holiday."

"Alexander Wade," he said offering his hand. "From Savannah, Georgia."

"Maggie Bisby." Her fingers were cool and dry. Even in the sparse light he noticed a spray of freckles across the back of her hand. A proper English girl with a fragile English complexion. Hence the straw hat.

"It smokes," she said.

"What?"

"Your Morris Mini. It smokes white exhaust. Derek thinks your block is cracked."

"Damn!" said Alex, taking a huge bite out of a corned beef sandwich the bar girl placed before him.

"He says if you keep driving it, you'll blow a head gasket."

He rolled his eyes and swallowed. "Wonderful! Just when I need it the most!"

"Are you on holiday too?"

"No, I live in Dublin." He glanced at his watch. "I've got a two-o'clock appointment with a man just down the road in Killiney."

"We're going that way," she said. "We could follow you, and if anything goes awry, we could give you a hitch, couldn't we." When she smiled, the bridge of her nose crinkled.

"Derek will be ecstatic with that plan."

"Derek will do as he is told." She drained her glass and slid off the stool.

Ten minutes later, with Maggie belted into his passenger seat, Alex prodded the old Mini out onto the Coast Road. Derek followed affably, the pretty blonde at his side.

"What's under the blanket?" Maggie asked.

"Canvases. Some stuff I've been working on."

"So you're a painter." She lifted his left hand from the steering wheel and inspected the fingers. "And this man in Killiney—is he going to buy your paintings?"

"That's the big question." Her direct inquisition made Alex uncomfortable; he wished she'd talk about something else.

"Is that why you're so tense?" She returned his hand to the wheel.

"Bisby," he said. My great great great grandmother was a Bisby. Wouldn't it be odd if it turned out we're cousins?"

But Maggie had leaned back against the headrest and closed her eyes. In profile her umber lashes swept over her cheek softening the straight angle of her nose. He decided she wasn't pretty in the traditional sense—like the blonde in the Porsche behind. "Arresting" was as close as he could come.

"There it is, number 1404," she said, pointing up ahead. She helped him unload the paper-wrapped canvases and carry them into Liam Thane's gallery. Then, waving away his thanks, she telescoped into the back seat of the red Porsche, which whipped around the corner and disappeared.

* * *

"Mr. Thane was very sorry to have to cancel," said his young assistant. "We tried to ring you up as soon as we knew, but your number wasn't listed."

"I don't have a telephone," said Alexander. His disappointment was palpable. So much depended upon Liam Thane's acceptance. Maybe too much, he decided.

"If you'd care to leave your canvases, Mr. Thane will contact you in a fortnight when he returns from London."

Alex didn't know which upset him more—that his anxiety must continue for another two weeks or that a whole day had been spent away from his easel to no avail.

He shoved the receipt for his paintings into the pocket of his jeans and slid behind the wheel of the Mini. Five kilometers beyond the King's Rook the engine faltered, and Alex knew Derek Bisby's dire predictions had come true. He limped off the highway as far as possible, locked the doors, and set off on foot, sticking out his thumb at every passing vehicle.

"Maybe it's an omen," he muttered not sure whether he believed in such things. Fatigue throbbed behind his eyes. He had hardly slept the night before so eager was he for this day, so hopeful. Considering how plans had gone awry, he should be depressed or, at the very least, pissed off. Instead he felt curiously buoyant, uplifted by the mocking gulls and the unencumbered freedom of his stride. "Isle of Wight, Isle of Wight," chanted his boots as he trudged along the gravel shoulder. The salt-breeze left a tang on his lips, and he gave in to an urge to whistle.

After nearly an hour, a lorry with a cargo of pigs pulled to a stop beside him. When the driver insisted on payment in advance, Alex doled out his last five euros without a quibble. They rode in silence back to Dublin and parted at the outskirts of the Coombe.

At least the day wasn't a total loss, thought Alex as he held his freezing hands to the flame beneath his teakettle. For awhile he had enjoyed the company of a green-eyed girl in a red Porsche. He wondered if he would ever see Maggie Bisby again.

*P*arts and labor plus €20 if you get it fixed by the end of the week," said Alexander, tossing him the keys.

Tim McCann grinned and squinted at him sideways. "Thirty, and it's a deal."

"Twenty-five, you Celtic bandido, and not a tuppence more."

"Done." Tim stooped to unfasten the towing chain from the frame of the Morris, and together they pushed it inside the single bay of McCann's Motor Service.

Tim lowered the overhead door and rubbed his hands on the seat of his greasy overalls. He shifted self-consciously from one foot to the other and squinted upward at a jet trail bisecting the afternoon sky.

"I'm having a few friends in tonight," he said, clearing his throat. "Why don't you stop by for a pint if you've nothing else planned."

Of the few people Alexander had met in Dublin, Tim came closest to being a friend. He lived alone in a Spartan flat one floor below Alexander and supported himself by perpetuating his dead father's auto repair service, a life he loathed. When he could afford it, Tim took night classes at Dublin's Dun Laoghaire College of Art and Design. But lack of funds and the demands of the garage often interfered. The two men occasionally ate supper together around the corner at The Lamb and Lion and talked about their art.

Until now Tim had been hesitant to include Alexander in his circle. A reclusive American with the time and means to pursue his muse, Alex was of a different breed.

He was caught off guard. "Well, I—that's really nice. Thanks."

"Good. About seven then," said Tim, looking slightly relieved. "Something I want to show you."

Alexander purchased several charcoal pencils and a fine sable brush from the artist's supply store on the corner, then jogged back to his flat to make the most of the late afternoon light.

Two envelopes awaited him on a small table in the vestibule. He shoved the one from his sister into his pocket and ripped open the other, reading as he mounted the stair.

April 23, 2004

Mr. Alexander T. Wade
27 Lower Meecham Lane
Dublin, Irish Republic

Dear Mr. Wade:

Please accept my apologies for canceling our appointment on such short notice. I hope it did not cause you undue inconvenience.

I have taken the liberty of showing your work to my friend and competitor, Arthur Dowd, whose judgement I value highly. He concurs that it shows great promise, particularly your life studies and portraiture. He will be contacting you soon to discuss commissioning a portrait for one of his clients. The benefit of Arthur Dowd's sponsorship can not be overemphasized.

Our mission, meanwhile, must be to present your work to Ireland and Great Britain. To that end, I propose including twenty of your best canvases in my gallery's fall show, sharing space with Helmut Schindler, a young artist from Berne, whose bold graphics stand in complementary contrast to your own more subtle hand. Let us plan another meeting — perhaps the first or second week in May?

I look forward to meeting you.

Yours,

Liam Thane
L. Thane Galleries
London - Dublin – Edinburgh

P.S. A client has expressed interest in the "Kirk of Corey." Let me know if you would be willing to sell it for €900.

Alexander let out a whoop and lunged toward a stack of canvases leaning against the wall. This one would do, and this one. But that one and several others needed modification, refinement. He would have less than five months to finish enough works in progress to have twenty ready for showing. Whenever would he find the time for a new commission?

Perhaps he'd better decline. Still, if Arthur Dowd was as influential as Thane indicated, he'd be a fool to let such an opportunity go by. Alex realized his hands were shaking with excitement; he sat back on his heels to catch his breath.

"Whiskey!" he declared, slapping his thigh. He pocketed his wallet and, grabbing a jacket from the hook behind his door, he bounded down the stairs two at a time. Tonight was to be a night for celebrating!

* * *

Tim McCann's door stood ajar, allowing the hard rock of The NecRomancers to pump at full volume into the hallway. A girl in tight jeans and lavender boots shouted a greeting to Alex and relieved him of his bottle of Tullamore Dew. She led him by the hand to a card table bar in one corner of the living room and disappeared into the kitchen.

Alexander filled a paper cup halfway with somebody else's whiskey and topped it off with water from a pitcher. He'd been in Ireland long enough not to expect ice.

A coal fire glowed in the grate warming the bare feet of a couple in matching ski sweaters. Between them sprawled an enormous Bouvier de Flandres, registering its approval with an occasional thump of its tail.

To Alex's relief, someone turned the volume down and substituted a CD of soft jazz. His host, who beckoned to him from a couch in the corner, sat beside a pretty blonde in a long denim skirt. Her face was vaguely familiar.

"Meet Sam Gray," said Tim. "Alex Wade, my neighbor." He slipped his arm around the girl's shoulder and gave it an affectionate squeeze. "Sam is the best auto mechanic I've ever worked with. I'll leave you two to get acquainted." As he stood, the girl doubled her fist and delivered him a playful punch, then turned blue eyes to Alex.

"Samantha," she smiled. "And I think we almost met once before." She moved over to make room for him on the cushion next to her.

"You're the girl at the King's Rook—Derek and Maggie Bisby's friend." Her hair had been different then, brushed up off the back of her neck and tied with a ribbon. Tonight it fell in a pale cascade to her shoulders. For the second time Alex noticed just how lovely she was. "An auto mechanic?"

"Not literally. That's just Tim's small joke. But he and I *have* worked together in a sense. He shares my studio."

"You're an artist?"

"Sculptor. Tim and I both work in metal—including automobile parts, which explains the joke. We met in a welding class. And Tim tells me you're a Yankee painter." She grinned at him, tossing the hair from her forehead.

"Don't let my Confederate ancestors hear you utter such blasphemy," he said smiling. "Where I come from, that's grounds for war! But before we do battle, can I get you a drink?"

"I'd rather dance." She smiled at him and held out one hand.

Sam was good—very good—and it didn't matter that Alex wasn't. Her rounded hips gyrated gracefully as her stockinged feet sketched a small pattern on the floor. He merely stood opposite, nodding to the beat and providing an occasional hand for her spin. They danced the next dance too, then joined some others at the bar for refills. Warmed by whiskey, Alex was enjoying himself, relaxing in the music, the firelight, and company of new friends.

"Got a minute?" asked Tim at his shoulder. "Something I'd like you to see."

He led Alex down a hallway toward a door at the end, and Sam, excited, danced along behind.

"It's not finished yet," he warned, wrestling with a padlock. "But almost."

At the flick of a wall switch, a spotlight shot toward the ceiling. Alex caught his breath as, suspended in air, a huge mobile rotated slowly on an invisible axis, piercing the room with little daggers of light. Each of its hundred fragments was chromed to collect and refract the light causing the entire sculpture to glow as if lit from within. It was dazzling, compelling, clearly a work of genius.

"My god," whispered Alex. "I don't know what to say."

"Three years of my life," said Tim. "And about four tons of scrap metal."

"Isn't it magnificent?" asked Sam. "Every time I look at it I see something I never noticed before. Where did you put that piece that gave you such trouble last week?"

"It replaced another," said Tim absently. "But I'm still not satisfied."

Sam slipped her arm around him and gave him a hug.

"Will you ever be?"

"Probably not. That's the essence of artistic madness. For every creative moth released by one's right brain, a destructive flame of self-doubt is ignited by one's left." He kissed her noisily on the cheek. "No wonder artists are such a schizophrenic lot."

"And our American friend?" she asked, turning to Alexander. "Is it like that for you, too?"

But Alex, moved both by the beauty of the mobile and the truth of the metaphor, was able only to return her smile.

"Dance with me," said Sam, taking his hand once more. They rejoined the others and eased into the slow tempo of Reno Moon.

> "I can see it now, your private smile,
> Can taste your tears,
> I can hear you say, I need you, Babe
> As morning nears . . ."

Sam's alto hum caressed his ear as he held her close, feeling lightheaded from the fragrance of her hair. Slender though she was, he could feel the strength of her shoulders through her soft sweater. He remembered being impressed with her handshake — a grip strengthened by handling a welding torch and a pair of blacksmith's tongs. Yet for all her muscle tone, she was graceful and womanly — a "lissome lass" Uncle Carter would have said.

As if she read his thoughts, Sam tilted her head back and smiled into his eyes. "Are you going to invite me upstairs to see your paintings?"

"Etchings," he laughed. "The line is 'to see my etchings.'"

"Ah, you're afraid!" she teased. "You're worried I'll play the flame to your moth."

"Not in the least. Come on."

The light was out in the third floor hall. Alex fumbled with his key.

"It's a mess," he warned.

"Don't worry. I shan't report you to the Eastern Health Board."

While Sam moved around the cluttered room perusing book titles and glancing at unfinished canvases, Alex rinsed out two mugs at the sink, noticing with amusement his sister Charlotte's unread letter in the dish drainer. If it were Charlotte poking about, he thought, I'd be trying to defend my "useless and unsanitary" lifestyle. But his guest was Sam Gray, a fellow artist who understood the priority uses of time and space and light, and he felt entirely comfortable with her here in his chaotic apartment. He poured them each a brandy, and then removed a stack of magazines and papers from a camp chair, motioning for her to sit.

From a closet he brought out four of his finished canvases and placed them in a semi-circle before her. Sam sat in silence, her face impassive, giving her full attention to each for long minutes before shifting to the next.

Alex waited with pounding heart, watching her closely for a sign. Approval? Disdain? Pity?

He sat cross-legged on the floor turning and turning his mug, trying not to sweat. He cast about for something witty to say to ease the pain of her rejection. But nothing would come. Light years passed; the plates of the earth shifted. At last she stood up abruptly and, crossing to him, dropped to her knees. She reached both arms around his neck and pulled him close. He held her, and they rocked gently back and forth in silence.

When she finally spoke, her voice was husky with emotion, and Alex, for all his mental preparation, was disarmed.

"Make love to me."

They turned to each other in his darkened bedroom and made a slow ritual of buttons and buckles. He tasted her mouth — flavored with brandy — and pulled the smooth satin of her body hard against his nakedness. They danced a different dance—this time to their own music, and again Sam was good. As if familiar with the clay of his body, she sculpted him with her lips, her tongue, her artist's fingers, firing his desire with her own. He, with gentle strokes, brushed her delicate rounds—breasts, hips, thighs—and closed his eyes to savor the colors of their passion. First a wash of violet, then a splash of magenta, and finally a wild, glorious burst of vermilion that left them both weak and weeping.

* * *

Whether the aroma of coffee or the clatter of dishes had awakened him, Alex couldn't be sure. But the prospect of breakfast with Sam both bolstered his ego and stimulated his appetite. God, he was hungry! He pulled on his jeans and padded barefoot to the kitchen. Sam, in his brown terrycloth robe, stood on one foot at the sink, her pale hair pulled back with a rubber band.

"You look like a lovely twelve-year-old," he said, nuzzling her neck.

"And you look very sexy—all bristly and rumpled and male." She kissed him lightly, then poured them each a mug of coffee.

"There's no telephone," she said, settling at the little wooden table. "Why not?"

"It didn't seem necessary, I guess."

"Don't you have friends?"

"Not many."

"Girlfriends?"

"No."

She made a project out of buttering a piece of toast,

beginning in the middle and spreading evenly first to one edge, then the next, rotating the plate.

"Somebody at home?"

"No."

She licked her thumb. "Then who's Charlotte Horner?"

He laughed. "What makes you ask?"

She pulled Charlotte's unopened letter from the bathrobe pocket and handed it to him, watching his expression.

But instead of Sam he saw Rachel Morganstern, a head taller than he and two years his senior. At seven she ignored him; at eight, she terrorized him. At eleven she stood before him offering to love him on condition he proved worthy. He must, without looking, reach his hand into the coffee can she held at arm's length and bring forth whatever he found there. Had he done so? For the life of him, he couldn't remember. But the intensity of her scrutiny etched itself into his memory forever. The child image faded, leaving behind only that look—of doubt, hope, fear, certainty—plowing gentle furrows across Sam's forehead.

"Is she beautiful?"

"Yes, I suppose so. A rather arch, brittle sort of beauty."

"Are you in love with her?"

"In love? Hardly! Sometimes I can barely tolerate her." He smiled at her. "Charlotte's my sister."

"You might've told me first off," she said with a playful pout.

"Now it's my turn. What's McCann to you?"

"Friend, soul mate, partner in crime. We tried being lovers once. It didn't work."

"And Derek Bisby?"

Samantha stared thoughtfully at her coffee mug,

caressing its rim with her little finger. When she looked at him a long moment later, her eyes were bright with tears. She took a deep breath and let it out slowly.

"Sorry, my guard was down." She pulled the robe closed at her throat and stood up. "I forgot you knew." He felt the pressure of her fingers against his shoulder. "You're a terrific artist, you know. Very sensitive, with just the right — touch. Last night I felt doubly honored." She tugged the rubber band from her hair and disappeared into the bedroom.

Alex absorbed the moment, chin in hand. That he cared about Sam was clear. What he couldn't decide was how to let her know there would be no strings attached to their friendship. The trust they had willingly invested in each other was enough. To expect or demand more seemed in violation of all that was natural and reasonable. He escaped to the shower, amazingly free of fatigue or hangover. As a matter of fact, he hadn't felt better in months.

He was buoyed by the sudden notion that Sam might be persuaded to sit for him. A profile would work — in natural light with her hair swept casually back and up. Perhaps he could do some preliminary sketches of her at work in her own studio just to get the feel of her.

The feel of her, he thought, and laughed aloud at himself. But as he was toweling dry, he heard the front door click. By the time he had wrapped himself up and run to the hall, she was gone.

The note on the pillow read:

"Call me when you get a telephone. Thanks for the dance. Sam."

Alexander pulled a rough wool sweater over his head

and combed his hair with his fingers. Then he poured himself another cup of coffee, added a bit of brandy for warmth, and carried it into the bedroom, whistling under his breath. For a moment he stood looking at the jumbled bedclothes, marveling at how different his life had become in just a few short hours. Reluctantly, he gave the blankets a tug, propped himself against the pillows, and slit open Charlotte's letter with a palette knife.

April 17, 2004
Savannah, Georgia

Dear Alex,

Let me begin with an overdue thank you for the lovely watercolor you sent Farley and me on our anniversary. We love it and have already hung it in a special place where we will be reminded of you. Someday soon I expect to be bragging about owning an original Alexander Wade.

I wish the other reason for this letter gave me as much pleasure. However, as your family correspondent, I feel responsible for keeping you updated on some rather unfortunate news regarding Aunt Olivia.

To put it bluntly, she is becoming senile and before long will most likely be incapable of managing on her own. Until recently hers was merely the eccentric behavior one expects from old people living alone. But now she quite clearly hallucinates — hears voices and talks to walls and maintains she "isn't alone" — that sort of thing.

Beau Harris (with whom I intend to consult next week) tells me she insists upon making her own decisions concerning financial matters. I consider her refusal to recognize the need to relinquish such control as evidence of her irrationality.

Also, I know, dear brother, how you feel about Lucy, and I agree she has served our family admirably. But our very indebtedness to her makes me uneasy, especially when I see her awful rag-tag relations hunkering around Aunt O. like wolves circling a wounded calf. Who can predict how those people might take advantage given the opportunity?

I am looking into various alternative homes for her and hope to find one where she can receive psychological as well as physical care. Meanwhile you could help by encouraging her to put her affairs into capable hands. Farley and I will gladly oversee her estate. We, unlike some anonymous trust officer at the bank, can be counted upon to keep her best interests at heart. There is no point in involving the courts in a competency hearing if we can avoid the inconvenience and expense.

Have fun, little brother. How I envy you sometimes — tearing about Europe without a care in the world.

Love,

Charlotte

Farley Horner lay supine next to his wife in the king-sized bed, snoring softly, his mouth ajar. Charlotte studied his face, which, in the mid-morning light, looked puffy and florid. Not a pretty sight, she thought. If I had to, I could identify his body with my eyes closed. Her fingers knew the exact depth of the indentation at the bridge of his nose, the texture of his chest hair, the angular planes of his kneecaps.

When had he acquired that gray tuft in his left ear? She tried to remember what she had found attractive in him. How extraordinary he had seemed with his boyish curls and boundless energy, despite being ten years older than she. Both families had been delighted by the match for different reasons. Farley's parents doted on their only child who remained a bachelor long after they had hoped for grandchildren. Ugh! Grandchildren! she thought. As for her side of the family, Aunt Olivia (though she never actually said so) was relieved to shift the responsibility for her troublesome niece to a strong man who obviously adored her.

Once upon a time Charlotte hadn't been able to get enough of Farley's muscled body. She sighed, remembering how she hungered for his infectious burst of laughter that made all things seem possible. Somewhere along the line, she had lost her appetite.

When Farley snorted and rolled over, clearly committed to his usual Saturday morning sleep-in, Charlotte swung out of bed and padded to the bathroom where she ran a brush through the tangles of her honey-blond hair. She searched in the bathroom mirror for lines and blemishes, and finding none, stepped into the shower.

Fifteen minutes later, dressed in shorts and a tank top, she grabbed her purse and flung herself behind the wheel of Farley's BMW. She knew he'd be annoyed when he woke up and found himself without a car, but her Honda was in the shop having the window repaired, and she needed a change of scene, an adventure, a fast drive to anywhere.

She clutched the sun-seared steering wheel tightly to control her morning-after tremors and welcomed the pain of its intense heat. What would it be like, she wondered with a small thrill, to be burned alive?

Her car sped east toward the islands through the corridor of Royal Palms along Victory Drive. Just last week one of them had toppled in a spring squall, crushing a Volkswagen and pinning the driver for several hours until the "jaws of life" could set him free. At last report, he was still in Candler Hospital, perhaps blinded for life. Charlotte shuddered. She couldn't live in darkness, couldn't imagine being unable to drive or coordinate her clothes or see her face in the mirror.

The tide was up she as she mounted the Memorial Bridge at Thunderbolt, and a shrimp boat chugged seaward on the Intracoastal Waterway. To her right sky-blue tidal pools studded the marsh grasses, while shades of green and gold ornamented the forest beyond.

Perhaps deafness would not be so bad. At least she wouldn't have to listen to everybody extolling the virtues of Saint Alexander.

As her speed increased, so did Charlotte's temper. She swerved to squash a lizard, but it scuttled to safety in the ditch. Even at thirty-eight she still felt the sting. How insensitive of her parents to expect her to be thrilled with a baby brother instead of the doll house they had promised for her eighth birthday. Before Alexander, Daddy took her everywhere with him, showing her off and calling her his little princess. They spent long afternoons together exploring the marsh in a bateau or flying kites on the beach. She delighted him by learning how to hit a clay pigeon with a shotgun twice her size. But a daughter was, she quickly learned, no substitute for a son. From the moment Alexander arrived on the scene, she could never recall having Daddy to herself again. Last night the dream had returned—the one about her father's discovery of baby Alexander's dismembered body stuffed in a box behind the furnace. At four a.m. she had awakened with her thumb in her mouth, plugging the hole in the dike, holding in the screams.

Charlotte seldom came to Tybee Island anymore, but as a child she had often enjoyed its tacky shops and tired cottages. She had thought the beach to be magic when each day's tide would reveal new treasures in the sand.

Her first bikini had been pink like the conch shell she kept on her dresser. That was the summer Joey Vandercamp sneaked up behind her and unfastened her top as she sat on a beach towel painting her nails. She went for his eyes, but he ducked just in time, getting instead only four red streaks of wet nail polish across his cheek. All he ever talked about was the Marines. Now he stumped around town on an artificial leg. Served him right, the creep.

Her white car slowed as it rounded the curve onto Butler Avenue and headed for the center of the village. On impulse, she pulled to a stop in front of Trader Jack's, drawing attention from a group of teenagers loitering nearby with ice cream cones.

"BMW — Big Money Wasted," snickered an overweight boy in a sleeveless sweatshirt.

"BMS — Big Mouth Slob," she retorted, stepping into the cool of the restaurant. As she selected a table near the window, a waitress in jeans and a Trader Jack tee brought her a glass of water and handed her a menu. "Breakfast?" the girl asked. Her name tag read "Joleen."

"Wheat toast and a small orange juice," said Charlotte, "with lime if you've got it." She waited until Joleen's back was turned, then palmed the small, silver flask she always carried in her purse. It held precisely 3.5 ounces of vodka — enough, she hoped, to take the edge off her hangover and see her through until lunch.

As she ate she gazed out the dirty window across the parking lot toward the beach, where happy sunbathers positioned their fold-up chairs and groped in their carryalls for towels and sunscreen. She thought again about the Tybee of her childhood before the glut of hotels and condominiums had ruined it forever while trying to make it into the Fort Lauderdale it would never be.

As far as she knew, only the cottages on the back river side remained unchanged. Slightly more weathered, perhaps, but otherwise the same as in the days when affluent Savannahians routinely escaped the heat of the city by taking up residence in their island homes, cooled by the breeze from the marsh. This early in the season, she knew, many of the cottages would be unoccupied. Charlotte tried to visualize what secrets lay behind their shuttered windows.

Although each bedroom door in her parents' beach house had been equipped with locks, the keys had long since disappeared. But by using the "key" from a tin of sardines, she discovered she could lock Alexander out. Then, with the heavy drapes closed against the sunlight, her room became a cave, a seraglio, a sanctuary. Sometimes she knelt at the altar of her dressing table observing her pious face framed by a makeshift veil. At other times she wept at the cruelty of her wicked stepmother and yearned for a handsome prince to free her from captivity.

Even at twelve, pain had intrigued her. Strapping her ankle tightly to her thigh with a belt, she hobbled about her room like an amputee, using a golf club as a crutch. She pretended nobody would ever love her, that she'd be a cripple begging for scraps in the streets. Once after such make-believe she found she couldn't unstrap the belt. Her face grew hot with the struggle as sharp pains shot through her knee and groin. She began to cry as her sweaty fingers struggled against the unyielding buckle. Finally, lightheaded and gasping in panic, she freed herself and lay panting on the floor, wondering if she was going to die. Both alarmed and fascinated by her brush with mutilation, she played the game often.

"Somethin' else, Hon?" asked Joleen.

"Just the check," said Charlotte.

Where had she read that mental illness sometimes makes people immune to pain—that they can hold their finger in a flame until the flesh curls and never even wince?

With satisfaction she noticed, as she shook the last few drops from the flask into her juice glass, that her own fingers no longer trembled.

Was it still there? she wondered. She knew she could find it if she tried. Daddy thought Alex's nightmares were caused by Mother's death, but she knew it was because of the severed finger in the pickle jar. He'd do anything — anything — to keep her from putting it in his bed after he was asleep. At first there was still some of Mr. Ames' blood and shreds of skin from the mower blade, but in a month it turned black like a sausage left too long on the grill. Mrs. Ames had looked all over for it hoping the doctors could sew it back on. Wasn't it she who had once recommended a psychiatrist for Charlotte? The old bat. If anyone in the family needed a shrink, it was Aunt Olivia!

Charlotte swallowed the last of her orange juice and reached into her wallet for some bills. It would be fun to dig up the pickle jar and send it to Mr. Ames for Christmas. Or maybe to Alexander.

"Thanks, Hon. You have a nice day," said the waitress, flashing Charlotte a smile. Her white teeth reminded Charlotte of Billy Crowder's white kitten that fell into his family's swimming pool when Charlotte was fifteen. She had been amazed how long the animal stayed afloat, crying in its tiny voice and clawing frantically at the tiled wall. According to her Mickey Mouse wristwatch, it took sixteen minutes and twenty-three seconds until the kitten went under for the last time.

The BMW would be an inferno, she knew, since she had again forgotten to crack open the windows. Instead she walked to the beach, slipped off her sandals, and waded into the shallow surf. In the late morning sunshine, she knew her delicate skin would burn quickly without sunscreen. But the cool of the salt water and the onshore breeze were impossible to resist.

A Labrador puppy loped past, with tongue lolling, and began digging in the sand. Its protruding ribs reminded Charlotte of the picture from *National Geographic* that her sixth grade teacher had passed around the class. The other kids thought the famine victims looked shocking and horrible, but to Charlotte their suffering made them beautiful — bony and fragile and close to God.

At first she had kept her vomiting a secret, but then her mother took her to Dr. Korbin, who hospitalized her. She liked her hipbones jutting out like rocks beneath the snow, liked having Daddy visit every day. Shortly thereafter her mother took her place in the hospital. When Abigail died, she looked just like the people in Miss Anthony's magazine.

Charlotte had started back toward the car when a softball stung her hard on the leg. "Guess what, you little shit," she shouted, grabbing the arm of the boy who ran to retrieve it. "This ball now belongs to me."

"I'm sorry," he whimpered, "It was an accident."

"No, *you* were the accident," she snarled, releasing him roughly. It was a line she had used before, hurled like a grenade at Alexander when he was six. How different life would have been had the "accident" of Alexander never taken place. Passing a dumpster on the way to her car, she tossed the softball in among the other rubbish.

In the stifling heat, Farley's car smelled of Farley — of bourbon and cigarettes and just a hint of cologne. He had smelled the same way last night when he came home at 11p.m. How dare he try to pull that old working-late-at-the-office crap with her. And how dare he suggest *she* was the one with the drinking problem!

"I've got to forgodsake *do* something," she said, smacking her hand on the wheel. "I need to *have* something of my very own." She checked her reflection in the rearview mirror and thought, What I've got to *do* is to *have* Hibiscus House.

*T*he telephone rang while she still had a mouthful of Lucy's walnut coffee cake. Olivia swallowed as quickly as she could and lifted the receiver.

"It's Charlotte, Auntie. How are you?"

"Just fine, thank you." The moment she recognized her niece's voice, she felt her shoulders tense defensively.

"That's good. Actually, I'm on my way out the door, but I wanted to check on your plans for tomorrow."

"Plans?"

"Yes, you know—Easter Sunday. I'm taking Farley's father to Bonaventure Cemetery, and we're hoping you'll join us. Then afterward we'll have an early supper here—out on the terrace if the weather is nice. Farley, of course, won't be joining us. One of his construction sites has flooded or something. But Dad Horner is looking forward to seeing you again."

Olivia stifled a groan. Besides being deaf as a stone, Harold Horner was the quintessential horse trader—a retired automobile salesman whose conversation seldom veered from the subject of deals, commissions, and trade-in values. Apparently, only she saw the irony in Harold's visiting his wife's grave as regularly as he had ignored her throughout their fifty-year marriage. Mary's obituary in the *Savannah Morning News* had hinted at heart failure, but Olivia privately suspected she'd heard about one spark plug too many and died of boredom.

"How kind of you to include me," said Olivia, feeling contrite. She worried about the ring of insincerity in her voice and wished with all her heart she had Carter's talent for diplomacy. He could always manage to state the truth without being offensive. She could almost hear him saying, "Thanks all the same, Charlie girl, but I'm sure Harold would prefer the company of someone with whom he has more in common." How she wished she could be firm and frank like that with Charlotte and not worry about it for days afterward! Why was she such a coward in front of her very own niece?

Because she frightens me.

In God's name, why?

She just does, Carter, I can't explain.

It had been a mistake not to tell him about the night Lucy's husband, Mr. Bates, found four-year-old Alexander, naked and hysterical, locked in the dark tool shed. Although Charlotte loudly protested her innocence, she offered no explanation for the fact that her jump rope had been used to tie the door shut. Terrified by her threats, the little victim refused to identify her tormentor and subsequently suffered screaming nightmares all through kindergarten.

While Olivia found the incident extremely disturbing, it was Charlotte's reaction to it — or rather lack thereof — that propelled her to the psychology section of the public library.

She spent several hours reading case studies of patients whose behavior mirrored Charlotte's.

Manipulative since birth, the child seemed to have no consideration for the feelings of others. Try as Olivia might, she could not recall a single incidence of genuine contrition, apology, or regret. Had Charlotte been genetically shortchanged in some way? Was it possible for children to be born without a conscience in the same manner that some lacked an immune system or adequate defense against solar rays? More to the point, could such a deficiency be cured? A hundred small incidents flashed through Olivia's mind, and she realized that the truth, camouflaged by the child's delicate beauty, had been there all along. "Sociopathic Personality" said the Encyclopedia Britannica — an unfamiliar term for a very familiar behavior pattern.

So here was Charlotte, twenty-six years after the tool shed episode, still manipulating, still unrepentant, still causing Olivia to feel wary and powerless. Aside from pleading an illness, which she had already denied, she could think of no gracious way to refuse her niece's invitation.

"That's fine then," said Charlotte. "We'll pick you up after church. Oh, and Auntie? Wear something pretty." She hung up.

So *that's* her game, thought Olivia. Good heavens, she's trying to play matchmaker! She punched the brocade couch pillow, furious with herself for acquiescing to such a preposterous plan.

Pulling on an old canvas hat, she went out to her garden to regain her composure and perhaps have a little nap while she waited for Lucy to arrive with the groceries.

* * *

"Blast!" thundered Cyrus, nearly catapulting Olivia over backward in her lawn chair.

"What on earth is the matter? I declare, you'll give me heart failure yet!"

"If it isn't one obscenity, it's another! Where is it all going to end?"

"Make sense," she snapped. "Where is what going to end?"

"As if it weren't painful enough to stand by helplessly watching William Goode's house being turned into a rabbit warren—now Captain Nugent's winter residence at the corner of Tattnall and Huntingdon is about to be ruined as well!"

"Please don't remind me," said Olivia sadly. "That's where Lucy lives. Ever since she told me about the 'For Sale' sign in front, I've been worrying about what will become of us if she has to move away." Her eyes followed the succession of little dust devils his pacing raised in the dry flower beds.

Cyrus "harrumphed" in annoyance, scattering a pair of Carolina wrens that had fluttered to rest in the branches. "How many happy hours Meg and I spent in the Nugent's drawing room," he said. "Never was there a more congenial gathering place for politicians and artists and men of letters. In the winter months their house was alive with music and conversation. Sometimes such evenings would last well beyond midnight until the coal fires could no longer stave off the chill. Then Meg and I would hurry home, too exhilarated to sleep. We would draw the bed curtains around us and talk until dawn."

In the crape myrtle a squirrel paused in mid-descent, then turned and scrambled skyward, scolding noisily.

"Nugent served beside me for seven years in the

Savannah Volunteer Guard," he said, his voice rising. "I defy anyone to name a gentleman of greater integrity or a soldier more gallant. By God, he took a sword through the belly in defense of our Confederacy! And now, in gratitude, a pack of filthy money-mongers is going to adulterate his house. Maybe even tear it down! How dare they do such a thing!" he shouted furiously. "How bloody well dare they!" His vehemence set the holly trees to trembling.

"Tear it down? But that's terrible!" gasped Olivia. Holly berries rained all around her, beating a tattoo on the patio table.

"I tell you, Olivia, if I were mortal again, I'd take a horsewhip to their backsides, damn me if I wouldn't!"

As if loosened by his furor, a limb came crashing down, striking the guttered roof and falling fifteen feet to the flagstone walk. Olivia leaped to her feet, knocking her straw hat askew.

"Good heavens, Cyrus, get hold of yourself!"

"You okay, Miz Livvy? What's goin' on out here?" Lucy stood at the garden gate, her arms full of groceries. She hurried through the debris and peered anxiously into her friend's face. "Who you talkin' to?"

"Why, I was talking to—I was just saying—Oh, dear, it's all so confusing! I must get Fowler's to come over and look at these trees. Why, I was very nearly struck by that branch!" She avoided looking at Lucy, whose black eyes darted suspiciously around the garden and then fixed on the old lady's face.

"Come inside now, and I'll make us some lemonade," said Lucy. "Then maybe you should go upstairs and rest awhile."

bsorbed by his work, Alexander was momentarily confused by the ring of his new telephone. Since his number had not yet appeared in the book, the caller could only be Samantha, Tim McCann, or someone wanting to sell him an electric duster. Or Liam Thane, he thought. He set his palette on the floor, wiped his hands on his overalls, and grabbed the receiver on the third ring.

"My name is Arthur Dowd," said a cultured voice. "I hope I haven't called at an awkward time."

"Not at all," said Alexander. "Mr. Thane told me I might be hearing from you." His palms began to sweat.

"Excellent," said Dowd. "Then perhaps you're already aware of the reason for my call. Let me say first off that I'm an admirer of your work—that which I've seen thus far—and am very much looking forward to meeting you. Unfortunately, I must be out of the country for several weeks, so that will have to wait. But as Thane probably mentioned, a client of mine, Julian Clarke, is eager to enlist your talent for a portrait of his daughter. As it is to be an anniversary gift for his wife, the project must begin rather promptly — he thought perhaps next Friday. Are you interested?"

"Yes, indeed. How shall I contact him?"

"Excellent," said Dowd again. "I'll send someone around immediately with a contract and some other particulars." When suddenly a pigeon fluttered to the sill and began pecking at the pane, Alex, giddy with good news, momentarily mistook it for the messenger.

"Let me just say" continued Arthur Dowd, "that Julian Clarke, aside from being a connoisseur of fine art, is also a man of considerable wealth and social influence. This commission could very well give significant impetus to your career." He coughed delicately. "If you feel I can be of further service in absentia, you must ring my office. My secretary will contact me." He wished Alex good luck and hung up.

At nine twenty Alex parked the front wheel of the Mini atop the curb in front of Sam's warehouse. He liked the abandoned look of the place in the streetlight, the heavy, utilitarian front door, and the hollow ring of his footsteps as he climbed iron steps to the loft. The light from a single bulb guided him past empty storerooms and unused offices to the back of the building where a small, ceramic mallet served as a knocker on a bright, orange door.

"Am I late?" He kissed her cheek.

"Very." She smiled at him and led the way to the kitchen, a curtained corner of the vast space that served as both living quarters and studio. She checked under the lid of a pot simmering on the stove, then poured them both a glass of jug wine.

Alex studied her pale hair with a combination of tenderness and objective detachment. Fragrant and silky to his touch, it refused to be duplicated on canvas. Her skin tones, on the other hand, had been accurate from the start. Except for her hair, Sam was a delight to paint, a natural model whose energy projected easily through her muscular grace. She enjoyed their work sessions as much as he, and often a whole afternoon would pass in silence, each preoccupied with his own muse.

Although the light was better in his flat, Alex agreed to set up his easel at her studio so her own work schedule would not be interrupted. In return she agreed to abandon her shapeless smock in favor of a leotard and tights. Occasionally, when business was slow, Tim closed McCann's Auto Service early and joined them, sometimes sketching at a drafting table, often fashioning metal shapes with a welding torch or on a lathe. Though the three of them never discussed it, a kinship had developed, a mutual respect that allowed criticism to be offered freely and confidences to be shared.

While neither Alex nor Sam regretted their first intimacy, neither sought to repeat it. Alex sensed that Sam, for all her cool exterior, was deeply in love with Derek Bisby and in agony at his casual response.

"What else could he possibly want?" she once asked, pacing back and forth in her bare feet. "I am talented, attractive, hardworking, honest— I'm kind to children and stray cats, I pay my own way, and I'm very good in bed. It can't be money—his family has millions." She launched a savage kick at a pillow. "I'm too damned good for him!" she yelled, bursting first into laughter and then into tears.

Tonight she was pensive. Sensing her need to talk, Alex leaned against the wall, sipped his wine, and said nothing. He understood the circular shape of her mind and knew that the maelstrom of her emotions would spin inward, eventually revealing the issue central to her mood.

"If you could be assured of one thing," she asked, "what would you choose?" Alex swirled his wine and thought about her question, not for the first time.

"You are the master of your fate," Mr. Crispin, his high school English teacher, had said, "the captain of your soul. If you neglect the helm, you'll wake up one morning and find yourself adrift." Even at sixteen, Alex had squirmed at the hackneyed metaphor. It was Carl Crispin's life, not his poetry, that reinforced the lesson and left an indelible mark. A copy of *The New York Times'* review of his first book, published the year of his graduation from Yale, hung in a cheap frame behind his desk. It proclaimed him a "bright, new star" from whom the world could expect "incisive social commentary." Marbury House paid him an impressive advance and shipped him off on a six-week promotional tour, from which, Alex knew, he had never fully returned. Forty years later his second book, written in an alcoholic haze, lay half-finished and curling at the edges.

"Life poses only one question, my boy," warned Mr. Crispin, raising a nicotined finger. "What single thing do you want before you die?"

"Validation," he told Sam.

"What sort of validation?"

"The kind that says to the world, 'This man is not a fraud, not an imposter. He is not perpetrating a hoax upon mankind. What he thinks and feels and paints is real, genuine, true, and therefore worthwhile. He deserves to be.'"

"Do you really doubt any of those things?"

"Every day of my life." He watched the play of light on her hair as she ladled out two bowls of stew and filled fresh glasses from the jug. By now Crispin would be seventy-seven — if he were still alive. But as master of his fate, would he choose to prolong such an inconsequential existence? Somehow Alex doubted it.

Sam motioned him toward a kitchen stool.

"What would you choose?" he asked.

She studied the napkin on her lap, then carefully smoothed it, intent upon aligning the edges. "When I was twelve, we lived on a hill in an old stone house that was too small for the likes of my family. There were eight of us — including my grandparents, who had fallen on hard times. It was right cold in that house and lonely, because the nearest village was five miles down the road.

"My schoolmates were townsfolk who looked down on country children, so I didn't have many friends." She sipped her wine, lost in another time, unaware that the music of her childhood brogue had slipped back into her speech.

"Once a girl in my form heard my father call me 'chicken,' and from then on they called me 'Biddy.' When I go back there, sometimes people still call me that. I don't mind now, but at twelve one barely survives such humiliation." Sam shot him a quick smile, then resumed her story, tracing the rim of her wine glass with one finger.

"Papa worked in a textile mill. I can still see him riding off to work on his terrible, old two-wheeler with his lunch in a pouch and his muffler wrapped 'round his neck. At five o'clock when the mill whistle blew, I would wait at an upstairs window watching for Papa to turn onto our road. He would burst into the house yelling, 'Any chickens in this coop?' I would come flying down the stairs calling, 'Here I am!' and fling myself into his arms. He smelled of tobacco and new cloth, and his beard felt stubbly against my cheek."

Sam rose to fetch a candle, touch a match to the wick, and carry it to the table. She settled again opposite Alexander and reached for his hand. "I can't imagine why I'm telling you all this boring lot."

"Not boring at all. Go on." He gave her hand a squeeze.

"One Sunday I drew a picture of Papa asleep on the grass with his arm around our old dog, Saffron. When the master at my school entered it in a competition and it won second place, Papa rode his bike to school and strutted around bragging to everyone that he was the model. I understood that it was his way of saying he was proud of me."

She upended her wine glass. "Pour me another, love, and one for yourself if you will."

"Go on."

"We weren't exactly poor, but there was little money for luxuries. So when Papa told me I could have a party to celebrate my thirteenth birthday, I was in a frenzy of excitement. I fretted over the guest list, my hair, my clothes. I changed the menu so many times that Grandmum threw up her hands and refused to have anything further to do with the project. I threatened my brothers lest they embarrass me and worried about the shabbiness of our house.

"Mum spent the whole day baking Victoria sponge rock and fairy cakes with rosettes of pink frosting. Papa brought home balloons, and we all sat around blowing and laughing until we were red in the face." She chuckled despite the hint of tears behind her eyes.

"Finally it was time. I remember standing before the mirror thinking that although I wasn't beautiful, there was a definite possibility I might one day be pretty. That gave me the confidence to face Eddie McGuire whom I desperately wanted to notice me."

"And did he?"

"He didn't come," she said. "Nobody came. I sat there in the window until ten o'clock, sick with disappointment. I fell asleep waiting, and Papa carried me to bed in my party dress. He was furious and wanted to march up to school demanding an explanation and an apology. But I was so terribly humiliated that I made him promise not to. We never found out who was responsible for such a cruel prank." Sam made an effort to steady her voice. "I still hurt from that experience, still fear abandonment by my friends. My worst dream is one in which I'm there but no one can see me because I'm invisible."

She wiped her eyes on her napkin and took a deep breath, giving Alexander a watery smile. "Derek makes me feel invisible like that," she said. "I want to shout at him, 'Here I am!' and run into his arms. But he looks beyond me or through me. He never really notices I'm there." She picked at the candle wax and fed it to the flame. "We're quite a team, you and I," she laughed without humor. "One of us in-valid and the other invisible."

Alex chucked the dishes in the sink and set the teakettle on the flame. He stood behind Sam with his arms around her, his cheek against her hair.

"Is he worth it?"

"Of course not. Logically, nobody is. But when has love ever had anything do to with logic?" She hiccupped softly, crying again. "Who can say what weird chemistry makes one person grab the heart of another? Derek is my — narcotic, and I am hooked."

"Where did you meet?"

"In a pub."

"When?"

"About three years ago. One evening after a ceramics

class, I went with some chums for a pint. Earlier that day an IRA bomb had exploded in a car park in Belfast, killing twelve or thirteen Christmas shoppers. Very intense, very full of ourselves, our group got to arguing politics — something one daren't do in Ireland if one wants to keep one's friends. It got nasty, and a brawl started. Derek, whom I hadn't met until that moment, grabbed me and hustled me out the door so I wouldn't get hurt. He drove me home in his Jaguar — he had a white one then — and I invited him up for coffee. He stayed for three days."

"Then what happened?"

"Nothing. That's the terrible part. I fell in love, and he didn't." She was pacing again. "Every few months he comes around, and we have a wonderful time together. He gets a kick out of buying me presents that I don't want or need; he takes me to elegant places and makes me feel like I belong. Wherever we go, people know him — maître d's, doormen, barkeeps . . . It's heady stuff. But when he's gone again, I try to recall our conversations, to remember something meaningful he said, and it's a blank. I can never decide if Derek is incredibly shallow or so deep that he's cerebrating on two levels at once and I'm privy only to the superficial one."

"Where does he go when he leaves?"

"Who knows. Maybe he has a string of lovers all over the British Isles that he visits on a rotating basis." Sam pulled a handful of tissues from a box beneath the counter. "His family has an estate on the Isle of Wight. I've never seen it, of course, but from what he's told me, it's quite wonderful. The house sits on a cliff overlooking the Solent. When they're not skiing at Innsbruck or sunning in the Canary Islands, his mother and stepfather spend a lot of time in America."

"Tell me about his sister," said Alex.

"I've only met Maggie a few times, but she seems a pleasant enough sort. She loves her brother even though she doesn't quite approve of him. I think she and I might be friends if we weren't from such different worlds."

Her demons temporarily dispelled, Sam curled up on the couch and accepted a cup of coffee from Alex. She sighed. "Have you ever been in love?"

"Yes, once, and it nearly destroyed me. Her name was Avis Longtree, and she had the biggest biceps in the fourth grade. One time she picked me up and slam dunked me into a trash basket. She terrified me. I worshipped her."

Sam's laughter ricocheted around the huge room.

"Now that you know all my secrets, I have to go home," said Alex. "This morning I learned that my patron's daughter will present herself at my door one day soon for a portrait sitting. I've got so much to do between now and my show in the fall, I'm feeling a little overwhelmed. Say something reassuring."

"You'll be terrific." Sam smiled into his eyes. "You are terrific."

*   *   *

Half an hour later Alex sat on the edge of his bed and slit open the envelope that had been shoved beneath his door. Below Arthur Dowd's engraved letterhead was a legal-looking document and a brief message in a strong hand.

Tuesday
Dear Mr. Wade:

Mr. Julian Clarke is delighted that you have agreed to accept his commission. He is quite prepared to pay for the quality he appreciates, and I have no doubt you'll be pleased with his offer. Providing you and your solicitor find the enclosed contract satisfactory, please sign both copies, retaining one for your files and returning the other to my office in the enclosed envelope. In the meantime, Mr. Clarke's daughter, Mary Margaret, prefers to begin her sessions on Monday of next week. If that is in conflict with your schedule, you may contact her at 01-807551. Otherwise, expect her promptly at 10 a.m.

Yours truly,

Arthur M. Dowd

*A*s the sloop *Rhapsody* motored past green marker 31 on the Intracoastal Waterway, her skipper locked down the tiller and moved aft to shorten the painter of the dinghy that danced along behind. Settled again at the helm, he popped open a can and saluted an egret standing sentry at the river's edge. He noticed neither the flutter of Olivia's white handkerchief nor the blue heron that rose from the marsh grass to escort *Rhapsody* around the bend.

Olivia pocketed the bit of lace-trimmed linen and found a seat on a fallen tree at the edge of the bluff. The tide had receded leaving an inner curve of river bottom naked and smooth as peanut butter. She resisted a girlish urge to fling off her shoes and run barefoot over its surface, to hunt for clams and watch fiddler crabs scuttle into their holes. The scent of marsh mud mingled with the perfume of wisteria, heavy and lavender like its bloom, and she breathed deeply, delaying the moment when she must rejoin the others for the ride back to town.

Why she had donned her prettiest blue dress and come

to Bonaventure Cemetery with Charlotte and her impossible father-in-law, Harold Horner, was a mystery. He had immediately embarrassed her by kissing her hand like some aging Lancelot and presenting her with an enormous Easter lily in a pink-foiled pot. Between them on the back seat had ridden its twin, ready to be placed beside Mary Horner's headstone. Identical lilies for two old fossils, thought Olivia. She regarded Easter lilies with the same loathing she reserved for all large, dramatic flora — amaryllis, birds of paradise, flamingo flowers, cannas. Only day lilies and poinsettias were exempt as they seemed not so egocentric. Give me a bed of pansies any day, thank you very much, she thought, issuing Harold a wooden smile.

Buoyed by an audience, he held forth throughout the entire trip recounting his heroism in the last hours of Mary's life.

"I gave her a pint of my own blood," he shouted amicably. "Type O-positive. I'd have given her a gallon if they had let me. But she was too far gone. The doctor said her heart couldn't take the strain, just couldn't take the strain."

"Perhaps it was her patience that couldn't take the strain," suggested Olivia in a tone too muted for his hearing aid to register. She rolled down the window to renew the air supply.

Charlotte had parked midway between the Horner and Thornheart burial plots. When Harold began helping his daughter-in-law unload a small spade and some bedding plants from the trunk, Olivia decided to spend a few private moments by Carter's grave. It was easy enough to find. How beautiful the statue of the "Melancholy Angel" was — just as lovely as the day twenty-nine years ago when she began her vigil. Only now mosses and lichen adorned her hair and her dress in delicate shades of rust and green. The figure stood atop marble base with a simple inscription:

MY HUSBAND

CARTER BISBY THORNHEART
1923 - 1975

She supposed she, too, should have thought of flowers, but somehow it seemed redundant. Carter had died on just such an April day as this, a highly inappropriate season for mourning. Now, as then, the old cemetery was lush with the new green of spring, its quiet avenues festive with white, red, and salmon azaleas. Spring beauties carpeted the copses, and nearby, wisteria spiraled up a dogwood, complementing its lace. She agreed with an exuberant mockingbird trilling overhead—the day was much too "vivibund" (as Cyrus would say) for entertaining somber thoughts. So she had wandered away to the riverbank to sit and watch the Wilmington River wending its way to the Atlantic.

A thread of poetry embroidered her reverie with its half-remembered rhyme:

> "But I have promises to keep,
> And miles to go before I sleep."

"Robert Frost," she pronounced triumphantly to herself. "Now what do you suppose made me think of that?"

"An interesting coincidence," said Cyrus, "since that's the very subject I wish to discuss with you."

"Robert Frost?"

"No, keeping promises."

Her sense of his nearness heightened when a small

lizard sunning lazily on the stone beside her skittered into the brush.

"I had forgotten what a pleasant view old Josiah Tattnall garnered for himself," said Cyrus.

"You knew him?"

"Yes. Our families were friends and distant relatives. I was about twenty when Josiah sold part of his Bonaventure plantation to the city for use as a cemetery. What irony that they kept the name. I doubt any of its current tenants would agree death is such 'good fortune.'"

Olivia felt his mood shift.

"Our first child is buried here," he said. "The headstone is gone from her tiny grave, but Annette lies beside her mother — beside us both." His voice faltered, and the breeze grew chill. After a moment he continued.

"Because we lost her shortly after the completion of Hibiscus House, we did not have a proper housewarming until the following year in 1858. We planned it to coincide with the unveiling of the fountain across the street in Forsyth Park. What a gala! The music and champagne flowed until dawn. To my relief, Meg exchanged her mourning clothes for a new turquoise gown. I remember her delight as a hundred doves were released to carry the message of peace to our northern enemies — a message that unfortunately fell upon deaf ears. Seeing her laugh again filled my heart with joy.

"Later that year, when it was confirmed that she was again with child, I took heart that we would realize our dream of filling Hibiscus House with happy children. Little Cyrus made our circle complete again."

"How brave," said Olivia, "to try again after suffering such heartbreak." Oh, my child, she thought. My perfect son. Stillborn with a thatch of black hair and long, curling eyelashes like his father. Perfect in every way except for breath. However did one go on believing in a benevolent God? "How brave," she said again.

"Yes, and determined, too, to nurture our child to manhood, healthy and secure. But when he was not yet two, she — she fell ill with fever and . . ." Olivia longed to comfort Cyrus. Her hand moved unbidden toward his voice.

"Several times throughout those last days I thought she was gone," he said, "but she rallied, each time more weakened than the last, as if a cruel God were toying with her life. Then one rainy night she called out to me as I dozed at her bedside. She was flushed, and her eyes were bright with fever. She pleaded with me to marry again, for she knew she would not live through the night. But I couldn't make such a promise. Instead, to ease her pain, I made another vow. I promised her that Hibiscus House would never be sold but would remain our family home down through the generations."

"And so it has," said Olivia, "as the portraits on the stair landing attest."

"But my great great grandson, Carter, was the last of the Thornheart line," he said gently. "Thus my present predicament."

The breeze loosened a lock of hair, which curled prettily on her collar. "However," said Olivia firmly, "the heirs of your great great granddaughter, Abigail, are young and strong. Neither is yet beyond the age of child-bearing."

"Dear Olivia, forgive an old soldier his insensitivity in bringing up such a disturbing subject. But my sand is running out. I have no time for wordplay, only for facts. Not once in his thirty years has my great great great grandson, Alexander, shown the slightest interest in finding a wife and fathering a family, so obsessed is he with replicating life, with mirroring its image instead of savoring its tangible pleasures."

"Yes, I suppose you're right. All the same—" She plucked absently at the petals of a wildflower, which fluttered to her feet like snowflakes. "You know, Cyrus, Charlotte seems determined that I move to a smaller residence, one more manageable for someone of my years. She even offered to 'look after' Hibiscus House for me, although I didn't like her tone." She tilted her face upward and closed her eyes with a sigh. "I suppose I should consider it. But, oh dear, my lovely garden, my blessed privacy!" Her voice quavered. "It's my home—all I have left of my life with Carter."

She pulled out the linen handkerchief and dabbed at her eyes. "All the same, I suppose Charlotte should have it."

"Not while I have one ounce of personification at my command!" he thundered. "Not until I have exhausted every means of manifestation! Not until my final evanescence is the only bloody option left!" A bit of the bank gave way, nearly unseating Olivia and sending an avalanche of stones tumbling into the river below.

"Cyrus, for heaven's sake!" she cried, steadying herself.

"I'm amazed, Olivia, that you, a woman of such keen perception, don't recognize Charlotte for the conniving wretch she is, that you don't see she'll stop at nothing to further her own self-interest, even to the point of doing you great personal harm!"

"I agree she's difficult—but surely you're exaggerating."

"It's not an exaggeration that she wants to use my house for her own purposes—to convert it into a tenement or a hostelry or some other abomination."

"How dreadful!" She rose in alarm and turned. Harold and Charlotte stood a few feet away gaping in amazement.

"And what's more—" yelled Cyrus.

"Hush!"

"Aunt Olivia, we heard you cry out. Are you ill?"

"What's more, she'll deceive you without conscience to get it away from you!"

"I— I can't discuss this just now."

"You can't discuss how you feel, Aunt Olivia?" Charlotte started toward her aunt.

"No, no, that's not what I—."

"Yes, yes!" continued Cyrus. "Deceive you, malign you, even declare you incompetent, if need be."

"She wouldn't!" said Olivia vehemently.

"Who wouldn't what?" asked Harold.

"Oh, gracious me," said Olivia. "I do feel a bit undone."

"That's precisely what the wretch wants," boomed Cyrus. "You're playing into her hands!"

"Into her hands," echoed Olivia, fumbling for her handkerchief. "Oh dear," she said again. "I think I need to— I just want to go home."

With Harold on one side and Charlotte on the other, they walked with her up the pathway amid the objections of an angry squirrel who chittered from above. They settled her in the back seat, then, exchanging glances, climbed into the front and headed for Whitaker Street.

* * *

"I'm sorry to call you at home on Easter Sunday," said Charlotte to Lucy on the phone, but my aunt overtaxed herself at the cemetery this afternoon, and I'm concerned about her state of mind. She seems even more confused and distraught than usual."

"Mercy me, Miz Charlotte. Lemme find my glasses, and I'm out the door."

Olivia eavesdropped from the stair top, then scuttled into her bedroom and shut the door.

"No wonder they think I'm addled," she complained. "So would I if I overheard an old lady talking to thin air! Cyrus, are you listening?" She stamped her foot. "You must promise never, never to befuddle me like that again!"

A few minutes later, Lucy knocked lightly, then peeked around the door.

"Brought you some sherry wine," she said. "And one for me too. We've both had us quite a day."

"Yes," sighed Olivia. "If I ever go anywhere near Harold Horner again, you must call Georgia Regional straight away and have me committed!"

Startled, Lucy sat down abruptly. "Miz Livvy, don't you be talking like that."

Olivia kicked off her shoes and, mindless of her Easter dress, stretched out on the four poster.

"What happened at your house?"

"Nothing. 'Cept Jonas heard the folks those real estate people brought over last Wednesday talkin' about offering $98,000 for it. They coming to see it again next week and take some measurements, and I'm thinkin' I better be somewhere else, or I might could shoot 'em dead when they step through the door!" She polished her glasses on the hem of her skirt, then wiped her eyes. "I'm glad Mr. Bates is dead so he don't have to see his family put out on Tattnall Street."

When Olivia didn't answer, Lucy assumed she had fallen asleep, so she tucked a soft quilt over her legs and tiptoed quietly away. But Olivia was far from asleep. Instead her mind spun with possibilities. Suddenly she sat bolt upright. Why not? she thought. Why bloody well not? I'll call Beau Harris first thing tomorrow morning.

A thunderclap jolted Alexander from sleep, followed immediately by a knock on his door. In his muzzy state, he envisioned his landlord—or worse, the police. Who else would arrive at this early hour? But a glance at his watch brought him suddenly to his feet. My god, he'd slept through his eight o'clock alarm, and now, at ten o'clock sharp, Miss Mary Margaret Clarke stood cooling her heels in the hall! Not only would she be appalled at the chaos of his studio, she would probably decide he was unreliable as well—not an auspicious beginning.

Alexander hopped barefoot toward the door, struggling to pull on his jeans. He had spent much of the prior evening worrying about what to do if she turned out to be homely. Would he be expected to improvise beauty where it didn't exist? He'd fallen asleep with the question unanswered, and now in the light of morning it seemed academic. A true artist could find something of beauty in anyone—a curve of the cheek, graceful hands. In fact, the greater the challenge, the more interesting the project. He almost hoped she would turn out to be unattractive, even obese. Quickly smoothing his sleep-rumpled curls, he shot the bolt and flung open the door.

She was neither.

In her bright yellow slicker and Wellingtons, she looked like a school girl dressed for a class outing, her small, freckled face half hidden by an oversized sou'wester. Panting from her rapid climb to the second floor, she grinned at him and held out a damp bakery box. She was charming. She was also familiar.

"Top o' the mornin'," said Maggie Bisby, stepping past him into the cluttered apartment. "I brought breakfast."

"I'll be damned!" he exclaimed. "All this time I have been expecting Mary Margaret Clarke."

"No wonder you look so undone," she laughed. "The Mary Margaret part is correct, although I'll refuse to answer if you call me that. Clarke is my stepfather's name. Sorry you were misled." She looked about for a vacant surface on which to set the box, then gave up and put it on the floor. "Go on, then, shut the door!"

Alex recovered himself and helped her off with her raincoat.

"My apologies for the mess. I had planned to do a bit of a clean-up this morning, but I accidentally overslept."

"Don't apologize, please. I shan't think any the less of you for it. Actually, I rather like the atmosphere." She grinned up at him. "Artists are supposed to be a disheveled lot, aren't they, leading a haphazard existence." She took off her hat and shook out her hair.

"Tell me, did your old Mini make it home that day?"

"As a matter of fact, no," said Alex. "But she's been

overhauled in the interim and is good for another 100,000 miles. Did I thank you for your help?"

"I'm sure you must have done. Do you have some tea? I'm freezing."

Alex filled his teakettle, his spirits soaring. What great good fortune to have Maggie Bisby sitting — well, standing — in his studio waiting for him to begin a portrait that would not only pay him handsomely but also afford him many hours of her company. He was torn between wanting to begin immediately and delaying as long as possible. He laughed at himself for worrying about what tactics to use coping with an unattractive model. From now on, his only concern would be to do justice to the magic of Maggie's face. Shoving aside papers and magazines, he offered her his one comfortable chair, then sat on the floor with his back against the wall, a sketch pad propped against his knees.

"Tell me about yourself," he said. "Maybe it'll help me get a feeling for the way to begin." He watched her slip off her boots and curl catlike into the armchair. Oh, this was going to be wonderful. She was lithe and supple, a natural model whose graceful movements were unplanned, unpredictable, and totally unself-conscious.

"I'm not very good at that," she sighed. "My life always seems like such a cliché. Poor little fatherless girl, bounced about from one home to another, from country to country — it's a poignant picture, don't you agree?" She coiled a long strand of auburn hair around one finger. "Except that I wasn't really fatherless, and I certainly wasn't poor! All those homes in England, Ireland, and France belong to us. It's true my own father died when I was an infant and my brother Derek was two, but he left Mummy a fortune in timberland, so our financial well-being was never an issue. She married

Julian Clarke a couple of years later and added his fortune to hers. Julian is a darling and the only father I have ever known. It's boiling."

"What?"

"Your kettle—it's boiling."

Alexander grabbed a towel from the kitchen table and removed the hissing teakettle from the flame. A moment later he handed her a mug of coffee laced with Irish Mist.

Maggie sampled the brew and groaned with pleasure. Like a naughty child, she plunged one finger into the middle of a cream-filled pastry, then popped it into her mouth.

"Now it's your turn," she demanded. "Start from the beginning. Who is Alexander Wade?"

"At fifteen I thought I knew. But the older I get the less certain I become."

"That's not fair," she pouted, once again impaling her pastry.

"Tell me what you want to know?"

"Something I haven't already learned through the grapevine."

"Perhaps you'd better fill me in."

"Well, I know you're from an old, established American family whose ancestry can be traced back to 18th century England. I also know you studied at the Sorbonne under Christoph Maxim, whose home you shared and whose children you tutored in English during your two-and-a-half years in Paris."

Alex was amazed. "You didn't learn all that from any grapevine!"

She squinted through long lashes. "Ve shpies haff our vays!" Her laughter reached out and gathered him in. "Actually, it's not very mysterious. When you mentioned your Paris experience to Liam Thane, he checked with his old friend Maxim and learned you had been one of his star pupils. About that time, Julian got the notion to have my portrait done, so Thane showed us your work and told us what he'd learned about your background. I must admit, I have avoided telling Julian your studio is here in the Coombe, or he might have objected to my coming alone. But the fact that I'd already met you was enough to reassure him." She smiled indulgently. "It took me a long time to understand Julian's protectiveness. It's not that he thinks I'm brainless — it's merely a matter of love. Julian would do anything for Derek and me." She took a sip from her mug. "Which is why, even at twenty-three, I would never go against his wishes. Why do you suppose I'm telling you all this?"

"Because you sense, correctly, that I really want to know. And the Coombe isn't dangerous — at least not this part — merely ugly and industrial and completely uninviting." He put down his sketch pad and helped himself to a pastry. Strange, he thought to himself, how comfortable he felt with Maggie, as if their brief meeting a month ago made them old friends.

Her eyes were lovely — large and green, slightly upturned at the corners. A full front pose would feature them best, but a profile would show off her graceful neck and shoulders. And how should she dress? Despite her slicker and jeans, she had the pastel look of a Mary Cassatt or perhaps a Degas, an eighteenth century beauty that might best be featured in something white and slightly old fashioned. He realized with a start that he'd been staring.

"Tuppence for your thoughts," she said.

"Strictly business," he lied. "I'm trying to decide on the best sort of costume. Have you any preferences?"

"Make me glamorous," she twinkled. "Make me wicked and sophisticated." She vamped for him. "Wouldn't Julian love it!"

Alex grinned. "If you can stand the chill," he said, "I think I'd like you to put on this model's drape so I can do some initial sketches in different poses. You can change in there."

Maggie saluted and disappeared into the bedroom. Moments later she was seated on a tall stool, her auburn hair sweeping across one creamy shoulder. Alex set to work in the soft morning light. His charcoal pencil flew across his sketch pad creating light and shadow with an economy of strokes. Every few minutes he'd change her pose: an elevation of the chin, a slight rotation of the torso, a shift of tension from one side to the other. He put the girl Maggie out of his mind and concentrated on decoding her physical message. After an hour, sheets of newsprint littered the floor all around him, yet he still wasn't satisfied. Something wasn't right.

He snugged a quilt around her shoulders and fixed them both another cup of coffee. Perhaps if he took a break, talked to her awhile, the answer would come.

"Why didn't you stay in Paris?" Maggie asked, sensing his frustration.

"A complicated question. I'm not sure I know the answer. Something to do with self-confidence, I think. Paris teems with talented painters determined to ignite the art world. The air vibrates with gossip about who's making it and who isn't. Fierce competition, to put it mildly." He ran his fingers through his unruly curls. "But it was more than that. Parisians are angular, intense, urbane. I hungered for fresh air and round, rural faces. In Ireland I found both those things — plus the anonymity to do as I please."

"Do you plan to stay here? "

"Haven't given it much thought," he replied. "What about you? Are you still on holiday?"

"As I mentioned, we have a home near Dunany up the coast. Sometimes the whole family summers here, but this year it's only Derek and I, at least for another month until our parents join us. We'll probably stay until October."

"And then?"

"And then I don't know. I've been giving some thought to going back to school. But where? And for what purpose? I've also thought I might like to start a business of some kind—a book store perhaps. I've a very good head for business. But Julian thinks I should experience more of the world before I tie myself down."

She shook a cramp from the hand that had borne her weight, and gazed out the rain-streaked window. Together they listened to the patter on the glass.

"I've never been to the United States," Maggie said. "What's it like, your Savannah?"

"Old, by American standards, and quite lovely. Lots of gardens and historic homes and wonderful old trees. Many Savannahians consider lineage to be more important than either money or political influence. We tend to be suspicious of newcomers and fiercely protective of our traditions." He stood and stretched.

"Southerners are a paradox," he said. "Gracious and hospitable on the one hand, jealous and closed-minded on the other. In Savannah gossip is a form of entertainment." He rummaged through a cluttered drawer for a razor blade to sharpen his charcoal pencil.

"Is it really tropical?"

"I've always enjoyed the climate. For nine months of

the year we live outdoors. But from the middle of June to the middle of September we hibernate in air-conditioned isolation where we regroup, reassess our priorities, realign our lives."

"And does your family agree?"

"My family," said Alex, "consists of one sister and an aunt, neither of whom has ever considered living anywhere else. Each copes with my gypsy nature in her own way. Charlotte sneers and Aunt Olivia defends and apologizes." He chuckled. "Leaving Savannah, you must understand, is tantamount to defecting to the enemy."

"How very odd," said Maggie. She, too, rose from the stool and stretched, letting the quilt fall to the floor. In thoughtful silence, she studied his sketches, her face impassive. Then she gathered the quilt around her again and folded up in the easy chair.

That's it! thought Alex. Her natural pose was to be curled around herself, private and self-contained as if protecting some secret from public scrutiny. Propping her on a stool with back erect intruded upon that privacy, allowing her mystery to dissipate. He grabbed his pad and sketched her as she was, a slight smile of satisfaction easing the furrow in his brow.

At two o'clock Maggie broke the spell. "I must go," she said. "I have to stop at the chemist's, and I promised Julian I'd have his car back by three."

Alex was astounded at the time. He had no idea they'd been working for nearly five hours, but Maggie was a patient model, and it was beginning to fall in place.

"When can you come again?"

"Friday."

"Not before?"

She smiled and touched his cheek. "I'll see you Friday at ten o'clock. Don't oversleep." She ran lightly down the stairs, her slicker over her arm. In a haze of happiness, Alexander heard the street door open, allowing the foul breath of industrial pollution to waft up the stairwell. Suddenly he leaped to his feet and bounded down two flights thinking, What a jackass—I should have walked her to her car! But by the time he reached the street door, Maggie had disappeared.

He sighed in self-disgust and trudged back upstairs, nagged by the thought that he may have just screwed up the luckiest day of his life.

According to an article his wife had clipped out of the *New York Times*, Beau Harris had it all. "Business Status — How Do You Rate?" equated corporate prestige with the inaccessibility of one's office and the expanse of its glass. From his wall of windows on the top floor of the Southern Trust Building, Beau could admire the graceful arcs of the Talmadge bridge spanning the Savannah River. He stood for a moment to watch a fully-laden container ship heading out to sea, then tugged at his cuffs and pushed the button on his intercom.

"Yes, Jean."

"Mrs. Thornheart to see you."

"Send her in please."

Beau rose as the door opened and greeted Olivia with a kiss on the cheek. "Good afternoon, Olivia. You're looking well. Are you enjoying this beautiful spring?"

"Yes, thank you, Beau. How is Dorothy?"

"Fine, fine. She's in Atlanta helping Lisa with our new granddaughter." He settled her in a soft leather arm chair and returned to his desk. "Now how can I be of service?"

"I need $100,000 dollars," said Olivia pulling off her white gloves.

A hint of surprise ruffled Beau's professional calm. "I see. Why such a large sum?"

"I wish to make a purchase. Immediately."

"May I ask what sort of purchase?"

"Yes, there's a house that's for sale for $98,000. I wish to buy it quickly—before anyone else does."

"Are you thinking of taking up residence there?"

"Oh my, no. It's not for me. It's for Lucy Bates, my housekeeper, who lives there. Her lease is being terminated because the house is for sale, and she and her family are going to have to move away."

Beau suppressed a smile. Even he, a Savannah boy, was astounded at the tenacity of the old tradition. The master still felt obliged to look after the servant.

"I know there is plenty more than that in Carter's trust fund," continued Olivia, "so if you'll just arrange for the bank to deposit $100,000 in my checking account, I can make my offer to Franklin and Hay Realty this afternoon."

"I'm afraid there may be a bit of a problem with that plan," said Beau. He buzzed for his secretary. "Jean, let me have the trust documents for Carter B. Thornheart. You see, Olivia, each trust fund is unique. Some provide more accessibility than others. If I recall correctly—thanks, Jean. Now let me see."

He selected a document from a thick file and studied it briefly.

"As I thought. Carter's will created four trusts—you are the sole beneficiary of one of them. There's one each for Alexander and Charlotte and a fourth for the maintenance of Hibiscus House, which, of course, belongs to you. Distributed income is, obviously, dependent upon the market. Since 1980 your trust has been generating between $50,000 and $55,000 per annum; Alexander's and Charlotte's roughly half that. For tax considerations the trust states that you may not invade the principal except for emergency purposes."

"But this *is* an emergency! Lucy is more than my housekeeper. She is my dearest friend. Why, if she moves away, she won't— I won't— I just can't let that happen!"

"Unfortunately, Olivia, the officers of the trust define 'emergency' as a health issue. If you were to become seriously ill, no expense would be spared on your behalf. But losing a housekeeper, no matter how affectionate the relationship, would not be perceived as an emergency."

Olivia shot out of her chair, knocking her hat awry. "What irony to call them 'trust funds' when in fact they represent the specific absence of trust!" She sat down abruptly. "Very well, if I can't be advanced $100,000 of my own money, then I shall borrow it. Surely Hibiscus House will be adequate collateral."

"That's true, Olivia, but in order to qualify for a loan, one must have regular employment or be able to demonstrate accessibility to other sufficient funds to repay it. In your case, your personal income would hardly enable you to make the kind of payments necessary to handle a loan of that dimension, collateral or no collateral." He rearranged small items on his desk top and cleared his throat. "It would be irresponsible of me as the Thornheart family's advisor on financial matters to endorse an action putting in jeopardy assets that will one day belong to your heirs." Moreover, Charlotte would have my balls, he added to himself.

"I see." Olivia placed the palms of her gloves together, carefully folding in the thumbs.

"I'm sorry I can't help you, Olivia." He leaned forward on his elbows, affecting a sympathetic expression. "But perhaps it's for the best. The world sometimes tends to take advantage of older people of means. We mustn't let our generous hearts rule our heads." He rose, squaring his shoulders and drawing himself up to his full six feet. "Let me know if your housekeeper leaves. I'm sure Dorothy can help you find a replacement."

"Thank you, but that won't be necessary," said Olivia. She closed her purse with an eloquent snap and walked out the door.

"Deliver me from aging belles," Beau said, tossing the Thornheart file on Jean's desk. "In their dotage they all want to play Lady Bountiful."

* * *

Olivia tipped the cab driver a quarter and, retrieving the mail from the box, unlocked the front door of Hibiscus House. She deposited her spectator pumps in the foyer and made a beeline for the pantry where she knew Alexander had stashed a bottle of vodka the last time he was home. Normally Olivia disapproved of drinking before six o'clock, drinking alone, and drinking vodka, but sometimes circumstances justified all three. This was one of those times.

She carried her glass out to the garden and sank into a patio chair, letting the music of the tiny fountain seep into her soul.

"Bless you, Carter, for this sanctuary," she said with a sigh. But she couldn't relax, so agitated was she by the uncertainty of things. Confident that the solution to Lucy's problem would be available to her through Beau Harris, she had not considered any other options. But now the cold, hard truth stared her in the face. If she couldn't come up with a lot of money in a hurry, Lucy would be out on the street. Olivia knew better than to offer refuge to the Bates family at Hibiscus House. The wound to Lucy's pride would not be worth the gesture, however sincerely made.

Perhaps she ought to approach Farley Horner for a loan; the construction business had been brisk this year, and Charlotte would, after all, inherit a substantial sum at Olivia's demise. But Olivia recoiled at the thought. Like many of her generation, the daughter of Elizabeth Gaylord had been taught to consider money high on the list of unseemly topics for genteel conversation, especially with someone who wasn't even "family." Furthermore, even if Farley *had* sufficient funds to underwrite the purchase of Lucy's house, she was disinclined to accept the emotional debt to Charlotte such a loan would impose.

Other than her engagement ring and the sapphire earrings Carter had given her as a wedding gift, Olivia had little jewelry to sell. And while a good many of the antique furnishings of Hibiscus House would fetch handsome sums, they weren't, as Beau had explained, hers to sell.

"Blast!" she said aloud, and smacked the umbrella table in irritation.

"My dear Olivia, you are beginning to sound like me," said Cyrus. "Whatever is the matter?"

"Must you always ambush me like that?" she snapped. "Couldn't you whistle first or something? Give me a bit of warning?"

"Very well, how's this?" He imitated a bobwhite.

"Perfect. Now if you're here to upset me with more

bad news, I don't need to hear it. I've had quite enough for one afternoon, thank you very much! What I *do* need is to find the solution to a very pressing problem. I'm facing a crisis, Cyrus, and I don't know what to do or where to turn." Against her will, her voice wobbled. "You wouldn't happen to have $100,000 hidden away somewhere, would you?"

"I can't even imagine such a sum!" he replied. "Have you looked in the wall safe?"

"Safe? What safe?"

"Behind the wainscot in the upstairs hall."

"I *do* seem to recall Carter mentioning something of the sort," she said, "but I don't think he told me where it was."

"Come along, I'll show you."

Through the oculus in the ceiling, the late afternoon sunlight dappled the Oriental stair carpet, worn and faded in places from the tread of too many feet. On the top step, Olivia paused, scanning the rectangular oak paneling that lined the lower third of the walls.

"Just there," said Cyrus, "at the end of the hall to the right of the bedroom door. See that small panel just like all the others along the wall? When you push hard on the upper left corner to release the catch, it swings open like a door."

Olivia found the panel and pushed, revealing the safe set in the wall behind. It was unlocked. It was also empty.

"What a disappointment," sighed Olivia. "Oh, I had so hoped it would be full of money and my worries would be over."

"Well, it was worth a try," said Cyrus apologetically.

"Hello!" called a voice from below. "Miz Livvy, you upstairs?"

"Good grief," muttered Olivia. "How did Jonas get in?" She started down, holding firmly to the railing.

"I thought I heard you talking," said Jonas. "Not like you to leave both the front and back doors open. Everything okay? You got somebody upstairs with you?"

"Dear me, yes—I mean no. I suppose I must have forgotten to lock behind me when I came home. What's that you're carrying?"

"Fresh eggs from the farmer's market. Mama asked me to bring them by and to see if you need anything for dinner." He kept a wary eye on the stairs.

"No, but thank you, Jonas, for taking such good care of me."

"Well, then, if everything's okay, I'll be on my way. Now be sure to lock this door behind me, Miz Livvy. And the garden door too."

"Eggs," muttered Olivia bolting the front door. "How can I even *think* of food with my stomach in such a knot!" She picked up her discarded shoes and, feeling quite light-headed from the vodka, padded toward her bedroom to lie down for a bit.

Shortly before midnight she awoke in terror hearing voices in the parlor below. Something heavy was being dragged across the floor, and a pounding noise reverberated through the house. Somewhere glass shattered. She pulled open her bedroom door and hurried out into the dark hall in her stocking feet. It was filled with smoke.

A figure with a flashlight appeared at the bottom of the stairs and began to ascend. Olivia, frozen with confusion and alarm, stood rooted to the floor.

"Out," commanded a man's voice. "We need to get you out. Are there others in the house?"

"No others," said Olivia in someone else's voice. She

winced at the sudden brilliance of the hall light. A man in a slicker and boots was steering her toward the stairs.

"What's burning?" asked Olivia, her voice rising. "Is my house on fire?"

"You got it," said the fireman. "You sure there's nobody else in the house?"

"Just my cat."

"I doubt it—not with all the doors open wide. Now watch your step, Missus. Have you got a coat?"

He grabbed an afghan off a chair and draped it around Olivia as he hustled her out the door onto the front sidewalk. A small cluster of people stood beyond the wrought iron fence craning their necks in curiosity.

Two chartreuse fire trucks with flashing lights were parked at the curb, and a huge hose ran alongside the house to the back. A fireman appeared on the piazza outside Olivia's bedroom window, leaned over the railing to inspect below, and re-entered through the window. She heard shouting from the garden and the sound of a siren approaching from the north.

The small crowd divided as a police car pulled to the curb in front of the first fire truck and two officers flung open the doors and strode up the walk, their radios crackling.

"You the lady of the house?" said the taller one.

"Yes, but I have no idea what's going on in there. They made me stand out here." Her teeth chattered with anxiety.

"Perhaps you'd be more comfortable in the car," said the second. He escorted Olivia through the gawkers and helped her into the back seat. "Now you just wait here," he said. "I'll check out the situation and be back to give you an update." He gave her shoulder a pat and closed the door.

She drew the afghan more tightly around her shoulders

and closed her eyes, not wishing to witness the frenzy of activity taking place in her front yard. "How could I have been so stupid?" she moaned.

"So intoxicated, you mean," accused Cyrus. "Don't you know women can't imbibe spirits without risking dire consequences? I tried every means in my power to rouse you—cold drafts, levitation, rattling—even singing falsetto at the top of my voice. But you slept right through it all. I guess some spirits are stronger than others, ha!"

"But if I was upstairs asleep, how did the fire start?"

"A young brigand slipped in through the back door and lit himself a candle to search for swag. While I was busy 'spooking' him—as you are wont to describe it—the wind from the open door tipped the candle into the waste bin, setting aflame the contents, which then ignited the window hangings. You do understand, Olivia, that if not for my vigilance, my house could have been destroyed!"

"I'm so ashamed," wailed Olivia, "and so grateful. Whatever would I do without you?"

Just then the car door opened, and the officer slid into the front seat. He transmitted a brief radio message to headquarters full of numbers in a language Olivia didn't understand. Then he half turned in his seat and smiled reassuringly.

"Doin' okay?" he asked.

"I'm terribly worried," she answered. "How bad is the fire?"

"Not bad. Some drapes are ruined and part of the carpet. Probably more smoke and water damage than actual burns. It looks like whoever broke in lit a candle to see his way around."

"Yes, I know," said Olivia. "I mean, that's what I supposed."

"Really!" said the officer, squinting at her oddly. "Well, anyway, the flame set the curtains on fire, which started the smoke alarm and scared him off. The firehouse received the signal about 11:30 and responded within four minutes." He tactfully avoided mentioning that the alarm had failed to alert her, assuming incorrectly that she had a hearing impairment. "Unfortunately, the intruder had time to clean out your safe. We'll need you to give us a report of its contents and a list of anything else that's missing. Are you the only resident?"

"Yes."

He wrote something on a clipboard. "Chief Howard says the front door was locked, so the burglar must have come in through the back. Funny thing is, there are no signs of breaking and entering."

"The safe was empty," said Olivia. "I left it open myself this afternoon." She drew in a sharp breath, and her heart sank as she remembered Jonas's warning. "I must have forgotten to lock the back door." She wanted to apologize to the officer for the trouble she had caused, for falling asleep, for being old and forgetful. But he was talking on his radio again, and her head was spinning. She felt dizzy and slightly faint. Missing? What might be missing? The silver coffee service? The crystal candelabra? The small Matisse in the foyer?

When the fire trucks pulled away, the tall officer followed her into the house and sat at the kitchen table to take a statement. He looked so boyish she felt she should offer him milk and cookies, but the fatigue in his face discouraged her. She felt foolish explaining that she had left the house unlocked while she took a six-hour nap, and could not bring herself to admit about the vodka. Charlotte's right, she thought. I *am* becoming a dotty, old lady.

The officer accompanied her on a tour of the house, its lower floors partly sodden and disarrayed from the fire. But except for the portable CD player that Alexander had given her, nothing else seemed to be missing.

"As soon as we've finished checking for fingerprints and found someone to board up your window, we'll be on our way," said the officer. He handed her a small card. "Call this number if you discover other missing items. And Mrs. Thornheart? Lock your doors!" He gave her shoulder a reassuring pat.

Olivia watched through the front window as he got into the police car beside his partner. Then she called Tomochichi inside, locked the door firmly, and went upstairs to run herself a hot bath. Perhaps if she sat in it long enough, the pounding in her chest would subside and she could forget how close she had come to destroying both herself and Hibiscus House.

livia's attention was so riveted on the display of framed diplomas in Dr. Milton Bluhm's waiting room that she jumped when he spoke her name.

"Mrs. Thornheart? Won't you please come in?"

She looked about at the chocolate walls and cream carpeting of his consultation room feeling tense and defensive. Should she sit on one of these chairs or lie down over there on the couch? How was one supposed to behave?

Dr. Bluhm smiled reassuringly and indicated a soft leather chair, then sat in another opposite hers. On a smoked glass coffee table between them were an exquisite Modigliani maquette and a squat bronze frog, their shapes and colors blending in subtle harmony. As she glanced around at the framed paintings—a subtle Feininger, a bright Kandinsky— she wondered where Dr. Bluhm kept his desk, files, and other "stuff of business," for clearly this room felt more like someone's parlor than the office of a "head shrinker," as Lucy would say. Even Dr. Bluhm, in his loafers and open-necked shirt, gave the appearance of a tall, slightly balding bachelor receiving a casual guest for afternoon tea.

"Would you like some coffee?" he asked.

"No thank you," Olivia said, feeling the tension in her shoulders begin to ease. All she had to do was relax and endure. In an hour she'd be on her way home again. Perhaps this interview that Dr. Patterson had arranged wouldn't be so awkward after all. Contrary to her mental image, Dr. Bluhm was not at all threatening, although she doubted that so young a person could be of any real help.

He smiled at her. "Very well then, tell me a little about Olivia Thornheart. You don't mind if I call you by your first name?"

Olivia did mind, but to say so would seem ungracious. "There's not much to tell," she began. "I was born in 1923 and have lived here all my life. I married a Savannah man who died some years ago. We had no children. Now I live alone on Whitaker Street in the house my husband's great great grandfather built."

"Hibiscus House," said Dr. Bluhm with a smile. "I know where it is. Your house has always been one of my favorites."

She fixed her eyes on the frog, which looked as if it might spring at her. "I nearly burned it down," she said, shocked at her own words. Sitting here in this stranger's presence sharing such a personal failing violated every dictum by which she had been raised. Elizabeth Gaylord had schooled her daughter well in the graceful art of conversation: to be vigilant against self-revelatory subjects, to subordinate one's interests to those of others. If his smile had not had that little lopsided quirk in one corner, if his nails were not quite so clean and square, she could have resisted. But his shoulders, a bit thin and hunched beneath his oxford-cloth shirt, gave him a sympathetic look. Perhaps she might indulge herself just this once.

"Why?" Dr. Bluhm asked.

"Oh, dear, I don't mean on purpose. I accidentally left the back door unlocked, and while I was asleep, someone got in and set the house on fire. Whoever it was stole my CD player."

"I trust the damage was not severe."

"It wasn't, thank the Lord."

Dr. Bluhm studied his shoes in thought. Nicely polished shoes, Olivia noted, taking a surreptitious peek at her own.

"Do you know why Dr. Patterson wanted you to talk with me?" he asked.

"Yes. I went to see him about getting some sleeping tablets as I haven't had a really good night's rest since the fire. I fall asleep promptly enough, but about 3 a.m. I wake up and can't get back to sleep. Dr. Patterson seems to thinks the problem is caused by emotional stress, and he's reluctant to prescribe a sedative until I've sought counseling."

"And do you agree?"

Olivia straightened her spine and brushed imaginary lint from her navy skirt. "I doubt there's anything wrong with me that couldn't be corrected by eight solid hours of uninterrupted rest."

"What do you do when you can't sleep?"

"I lie there and wait for dawn. Occasionally, I get up and read or write letters."

"Do you have any recurring concerns?"

"Sometimes."

"Would you care to share them with me?"

Olivia felt her face flush. She knew this nice young

man was a trained professional—Dr. Patterson wouldn't have recommended him if his ability were in question. But he reminded her so much of Alexander, so concerned and earnest, that she could hardly bring herself to burden him with her upsetting thoughts. Especially since he looked like he could use a good night's sleep himself.

"Such as—am I losing my faculties? Am I becoming a burden to my family and friends? Should I do as my niece wishes and resettle in a retirement home?" She regretted the uncontrollable wobble to her chin.

"What makes you question your—mental equilibrium?"

"I'd rather not say."

Dr. Bluhm leaned forward, his elbows on his knees. "You know, Olivia, talking about problems is one effective means of solving them. If you'll just speak openly with me—say what's on your mind—perhaps we'll find a way to help you sleep." He removed his glasses and squeezed the bridge of his nose. "I assure you that every word you say in this room remains in confidence." He leaned back, allowing the silence to accumulate in the corners, to pile up like sandbags against the walls.

Olivia was supremely uncomfortable. She had already confessed to being old and irresponsible. If she were to confide in Dr. Bluhm about Cyrus, wouldn't he, like Charlotte and Harold Horner and Charlotte's friend, Mary what's-her-name, and maybe even Lucy, conclude she was crazy? Would he, after all, be right? She breathed deeply to quell the panic niggling at the base of her skull. It all began with Cyrus, she thought. Not until he appeared did I ever doubt my own sanity. But he seems so real! Could it possibly be he's just a product of my imagination, a symptom of my disintegrating mind? She shuddered involuntarily, her right hand tugging at her left. What would become of her if she confided in Dr. Bluhm? More to the point, what would become of her if she did not?

"It's because of Cyrus!" she blurted. Her hand flew to her mouth. Now she had done it. No turning back.

"And Cyrus is—?"

Olivia bit her lip. "Oh dear me," she said in a tiny voice. "How very awkward this is!"

Over-prompting may heighten anxiety and undermine essential patient confidence quoted Milton to himself from some long forgotten text. Even without the reminder, he knew that emotional pressures, given sufficient silence and opportunity, would seek release. Dr. Bluhm said nothing.

Olivia swallowed hard. "Cyrus Morton Thornheart is— was—my husband's great great grandfather who died in 1879," she began. "Now he, or rather his ghost, has returned to haunt my house!"

If Milton had learned nothing else as the only 12-year-old Jew at a Gentile tennis camp, it was to allow himself never again to be caught with his guard down. To this day he made a practice of anticipating the unexpected and being prepared for it, a life strategy that had proven successful both in his marriage and in his practice. Thus, despite a moment of surprise, when Olivia's confession came, Milton was ready.

"So," he said evenly. "Tell me about Cyrus."

"He has a problem, you see, and can't evaporate (or whatever it is he wants to do) unless he resolves it, and he's got it in his mind that I can help him, but I don't know what to do, and in the meantime he's hanging around getting me all mixed up and making me say things that sound crazy to people who happen to hear me talking to him because they can't. Hear him, I mean. Anyway I haven't heard from Cyrus since the night of the fire, yet I don't know why because his problem still isn't solved, but the confusing thing is I can't decide which worries me most—that he might be gone for good or that he bloody well might *not!*" Olivia sagged against the back of her chair and blotted her forehead with her handkerchief. She felt giddy and strangled, as if a half-formed giggle had lodged in her throat. Dr. Bluhm fetched her a glass of water from a carafe and waited quietly while she drank, giving her time to compose herself.

"What is, uh, Cyrus' problem?" he asked.

"He promised his wife on her deathbed that Hibiscus House would always remain the family home," she said. "Yet I'm the last of the line except for my unmarried nephew, Alexander, who lives abroad, and his sister, Charlotte, who is thirty-eight and childless. Since they both have other homes, other lives, Hibiscus House will probably be sold when I die and the proceeds divided equally between them. Who knows what the buyer will do—convert it into condos or tear it down." A single tear seeped from the corner of her left eye and snaked down her wrinkled cheek.

"At least if I'm dead," she said matter-of-factly, "I won't have to watch it happen. At least *I* haven't any unfulfilled promises!"

Accustomed as he was to people in trouble, Bluhm was clearly touched by her distress. His conflicted expression suggested that while for him spending time alone held infinite appeal, he was also aware that too much solitude could, like an excess of Mozart, overwhelm the senses.

"Do you attend church, Olivia?" he asked gently.

"Not regularly," she replied, fidgeting with her purse strap.

"Do you belong to a bridge club or a garden club?"

"No. Why?"

"Because sometimes when we are alone too much, our perception of the world becomes distorted. Man is by nature a gregarious animal, you know, that often reacts negatively to prolonged isolation. It's possible the presence you feel in Hibiscus House, as well as your insomnia, is symptomatic of loneliness, of too much time on your hands and not enough human companionship." He smiled reassuringly. "When lonely children invent playmates, we consider it a perfectly natural part of childhood, but for some reason when adults do it, we view such behavior with alarm. Assuaging one's loneliness by talking to oneself is neither crazy nor unnatural — merely the mind's attempt to fulfill a human need."

"So you think I've invented Cyrus as a *playmate!*"

"I'm merely suggesting that instead of taking medication for sleeplessness that you take a bit of exercise, have some fun, perhaps do volunteer work at the hospital or get involved with the Red Cross. Push yourself to get out more, Olivia. Seek the company of others, and my best guess is that in a week Cyrus will disappear and you'll be sleeping like a babe."

But Olivia was not satisfied. Despite her better judgment, she had opened her heart to this young man, and she would almost rather that he diagnose her as senile than dismiss her anxiety with a palliative.

"Dr. Bluhm," she began, her posture erect. "I'm not doubting for a minute that you know your business. Perhaps you're right — that I'm imagining that my house is haunted because I haven't enough else to do. But if that's the case, explain to me how I was able to find my husband's safe that I had never seen before unless I was following Cyrus' directions."

"Probably," said Dr. Bluhm gently, "you filed away the knowledge of its location in your subconscious during your husband's lifetime, and only when something urgent triggered the need did you choose to access that information."

"Then how did I come to know all about Cyrus's life — that he married his distant cousin and was a soldier and had a baby that died and . . ."

"You are obviously intelligent, Olivia. As you demonstrated by finding the safe, you have an excellent memory for details. You've no doubt read about your husband's family's history somewhere, am I right?"

"Yes, but . . ."

"With little else to occupy your active imagination, you have embroidered the story to suit yourself, created an elaborate network of personalities to keep you company. Think back, Olivia. Has anything occurred since your ghost appeared that can't be explained in some other way?" When she didn't respond, he rose and hitched up his trousers, a boyish gesture that reminded Olivia of the generational gulf between them.

"Now tonight, before you go to sleep, I want you to start making a list of all the things you can do well. Then from that list select three that you can parlay into some kind of social activity — sewing, for instance — joining a quilting group."

Olivia collected her purse and drew herself to her feet. She took her time pulling on her gloves, stroking each finger carefully from tip to base, smoothing the fabric free of wrinkles, tugging at the hemstitched cuff. With equal care, she selected her tone and her words.

"Do you attend temple, Dr. Bluhm?"

He grinned sheepishly. "I guess turnabout's fair play. I don't go often—sometimes at Rosh Hashanah or Yom Kippur. Why do you ask?"

"I wondered if you believed in anything—unearthly."

Milton's face flushed. He offered her his hand.

"I've enjoyed meeting you, Olivia," he said. "Let's talk again."

When his patient had gone, Dr. Bluhm turned on his tape recorder and dictated a file report summarizing Olivia's hallucinations and enumerating the reasons why he disagreed with Dr. Patterson and Olivia's niece that her hallucinations were evidence of senile dementia—an opinion he would communicate to his colleague as soon as possible.

If Mrs. Horner were to proceed with her intentions to seek a competency hearing, he wanted his position clear and on record.

A pre-squall gust from the southwest eddied the dust in the gutter and swayed the huge live oak in front of 529 Tattnall Street. As Charlotte maneuvered her Honda into a parking space, huge drops of rain plastered a crudely crayoned school paper against her windshield. Like Confederate soldiers after the battle of Appomattox, a row of "m's" marched in ragged formation across the page.

She turned off the ignition and looked around for Mary Finn. Checking the time, Charlotte studied Lucy's house through the rain-streaked window. Kind of a dump at first glance. But the building did have nice proportions—fairly simple lines for 1870 and not a lot of gingerbread. Amazing that people would pay $98,000 for a run-down house that would cost another $100,000 to restore. Yet Mary Finn was sure she could sell it, and Charlotte knew it was in her own best interest to help her friend do just that. She was sure she could get Aunt Olivia into Three Palms once Lucy Bates was out of the picture. With luck, she could participate in this little charade and still be home by the time Farley pronounced the "sun over the yardarm" (whatever that was) and started mixing cocktails. She drummed her fingernails on the steering wheel, impatient for the time when, by pre-arrangement, she would walk up to the front door — too early for either Jonas or Lucy to be home from work.

At precisely 4:10, Charlotte saw Mary Finn's Lexus turn the corner and pull to a stop. She quickly gathered her purse and keys, pivoted her long legs to the pavement, and arrived at Lucy's front door simultaneously with Mary Finn and a stout middle-aged couple with a poodle.

"Oh, Mrs. Horner," said Mary Finn, faking surprise. "Please meet Mr. and Mrs. Arnold Smally. Have we, uh, miscommunicated? Our appointment was for 5:30."

"I couldn't wait," said Charlotte, wiggling with feigned excitement. "I've had my eye on this house for years, and I'm just dying to see the interior."

"But, Mrs. Horner, I've promised to show it to Mr. and Mrs. Smally, who have driven all the way from Illinois expressly for this purpose. I'm afraid I'll have to ask you to wait until 5:30."

Charlotte's face fell. "Oh, of course. I understand completely." She started to leave, then turned back, her face the picture of determination. "But please keep in mind, Miss Hagin, that I'm quite prepared to make you an offer immediately if I like what I see." She nodded to the Smallys and hurried back to her car.

* * *

Three hours later when Mary Finn picked up the telephone, she was still sifting through the events of the afternoon. "It was the damnedest thing," she told Charlotte.

"From the moment we stepped into that house, it was as if we weren't supposed to be there."

"What happened?" Charlotte wiped some suds from the receiver and submerged until she could feel the bubble bath on the nape of her neck.

"It's hard to explain—just a feeling I had. But Mrs. Smally felt it too. At one point she half-jokingly said, 'I think the poltergeists disapprove of us.' It gave me the weirdest feeling."

"So tell me what happened!" Charlotte said, perching her vodka and tonic on the edge of the tub.

"Well, first of all you remember that stupid little dog of theirs? When Mrs. Smally started to step into the house, the animal went crazy — yapping and hanging back and running around in circles. She finally had to drag him stiff-legged through the door by his leash. After a few minutes he sort of calmed down, but the whole time we were there he was skittish and jittery. Both Smallys said he'd never acted that that way before."

"What *is* it with fat people and poodles?" said Charlotte, sipping from her glass.

"But that's nothing compared to what happened next. Get this: We're standing in the foyer, and I'm going through my routine pointing out the paneling and plaster moldings when all of a sudden the ceiling light—a sort of lantern on a chain—begins to sway a little for no apparent reason."

"Maybe somebody was walking around upstairs," offered Charlotte.

"Nope," said Mary Finn. "Nobody was home—I checked. Anyway, next Mr. Smally goes down to see the cellar while Mrs. Smally and I go upstairs. It's a wonderful old house, Charlotte, with a nice staircase in front and an enclosed servants' stair in back. Every room has a fireplace and— well, anyway, we go up the back way, which is kind of dark, but when we get to the top, the door is locked. Mrs. S. tries her best to open it, and so do I, but it won't budge. So we grope our way down again thinking we'll go up the front way. But the door at the bottom has swung closed and won't open either. So we have to stand there, banging and shouting for Mr. Smally, who seems to have disappeared. Finally, after about ten minutes, Jonas Bates comes home, hears us calling, and lets us out. The strange thing is, the locks on both doors have been painted over so many times they can't possibly function. I inspected them both. And when we went upstairs a second time with Jonas, both opened easily—no problem. It was the damnedest thing!"

Charlotte inspected her toenail polish. "You must be making this up," she said.

"Don't I wish! But listen to this. We are standing out in the garden looking at the back of the house when suddenly Mrs. Smally gives out a little shriek. I turn around to see what's wrong, and she's staring gap-mouthed at the back porch where this old wooden swing is moving back and forth all of its own accord, and by this time she's really spooked!"

"Where was the poodle?"

"In Mrs. Smally's arms."

"Probably just the wind."

"Charlotte, have you stepped outside in the last few hours? Ever since that little squall came through about 4:30, it's been still as a tomb. Not so much as a leaf moved for the rest of the afternoon!"

"Sounds like someone was playing practical jokes."

"I know, but who? Jonas was standing right there in the

yard with us, and he was still with us when the Smally's horn got stuck out in front. What a racket! I thought we'd *never* get it to stop. By the time Mrs. Smally found her keys and Jonas figured out how to open the hood, it stopped of its own accord. We had drawn quite a crowd — including a reporter and camera crew from Channel 3 News. It wasn't until the commotion died down that we realized Mr. Smally was nowhere to be found. After a fifteen minute search, we found him down in the cellar — out cold."

"How did *that* happen?" Charlotte drained her glass.

"We still don't know for sure. He was very groggy when he started to come to and mumbled something about a sword — about getting away from a sword — as if he was scared or something. But we couldn't figure out what frightened him. The only sword we could find was in a dusty old portrait leaning up against the cellar wall, but why a painting of a Confederate soldier should frighten a grown man is beyond me. By the time he was fully conscious, he didn't remember what he'd been mumbling about. He had been poking around looking at the plumbing and the wiring when all the lights went out. He groped around until he found the steps, but halfway up his shoe got stuck somehow, and he lost his balance. He must have hit his head pretty hard to knock himself senseless."

"How do you explain it?" asked Charlotte, turning on the hot water tap with her toe.

"I don't know — poltergeists?"

"You don't believe that stuff any more than I do."

"No, but I think the Smallys believe it. Especially after Rose Smally's experience in the powder room."

"There's more?" laughed Charlotte.

"The best is yet to come. So we've been there for about

an hour and are about to leave when Rose has to use the facility. Mr. Smally and the dog and I decide to wait for her out on the front steps. We wait and wait and no Mrs. Smally. He finally hands me the leash — talk about freak out! I thought that little rodent was going to have a coronary! — and he goes in to see what's delaying his wife. First I hear her sobbing something through the door and him saying 'Push *up*, Rose, on the count of three: one, two, *three!*' I started to go back in to see what's going on, but Mr. Smally waved me away.

"Apparently, the woman has somehow got herself stuck on the commode and can't get off! Mrs. Smally, you remember, weighs about 300 lbs. She's beginning to panic, and Mr. Smally is swearing and sweating and yelling at her to stay calm, and the rodent is shrieking and running in circles winding his leash around my legs, and all of a sudden for no reason at all — on goes the smoke alarm!"

Charlotte let out a whoop. "Then what?"

"I fling the leash over the newel post, and the three of us scuttle off in different directions sniffing for the smoke that Mr. Smally is positive he smells. We don't find anything, but Jonas decides, just to be on the safe side, to call the fire department. Arnold Smally, meanwhile, drags a kitchen stool into the hall so he can climb up and shut off the damned alarm — God, those things could raise the dead! He's no lightweight either, and sure enough, the stool collapses. He goes over backwards and lands on top of the dog who lets out a yelp and pees all over himself, Mr. Smally, and the carpet.

"Just then the fire trucks come screaming down the street, and a good thing, too. The firemen manage to shut off the smoke alarm and free Mrs. Smally, who by now is hysterical.

Without another word, Mr. Smally grabs the rodent, bundles his wife off to the car, and drives away. That," says Mary Finn with a sigh, "was an unforgettable afternoon!"

"What do you know," laughed Charlotte, wiping her eyes. "A real, 21st century *haunting* right here in our own backyard!"

* * *

"Hee, hee, hee," chortled Cyrus. His little dance of glee caused static electricity to spark from Olivia's oriental rug. Even her hands-on-hips pose couldn't neutralize his fiendish pleasure.

"It was you, wasn't it!" she demanded. "When Jonas told me what had happened to those poor people, I thought to myself the whole thing sounded suspiciously like a Cyrus Thornheart special. You should be ashamed of yourself!"

"It's all part of the plan, Olivia" he assured her. "Actually you would have enjoyed the performance. Very deft I've become, if I do say so myself. A first-rate haunting, that's what you would have witnessed this afternoon, ha!"

As it expanded, the grey-beige stain on the ceiling took the shape of a monk in hooded robe, ominous and sinister in the early morning light. Thirty minutes later it had transformed itself into the profile of a toothless crone. Rain ping-pinged into a saucepan at the foot of the bed where Alexander, his right arm and hand numbed with paralysis, lay contemplating the rest of his life. It seemed unlikely, lying there in the bone-chilling cold of his squalid room, that he would ever again be so happy as he was at this moment.

He thought back to the beginning, to another rainy morning not so long ago when a knock on his door changed his luck — his life — forever. One great, warm tear of pleasure escaped from his right eye and pinged, like the rain, onto Maggie's cheek. She stirred and snuggled closer, sending prickles of sensation skittering toward his shoulder.

As the slow-motion explosion on the ceiling sent the hag up in a mushroom cloud, he thought of the incredible coincidence that had brought them together. What if the Morris had broken down a day earlier? What if he had taken a different route to the King's Rook pub? What if . . . But it hadn't and he hadn't, and now she was here with her head on his shoulder, her fragrant hair fanned out across her breast. She was fragile yet strong, this love of his, in whose husky laugh echoed the most erotic music in the universe.

"Chocolate pie," she mumbled in a sleepy voice.

"Hmm?"

"I could eat a whole chocolate pie for breakfast."

Alexander tightened his arms around her and kissed the top of her head. "We'll order one from Grady's—no, two. One for each of us."

She threw back the covers and stretched luxuriously, enjoying the caress of his eyes.

"Are you that generous with all your women?" she laughed.

"Only those with freckles."

At noon when he awoke again, Alex purposefully set the kettle on the fire and stepped into the shower. Anxiety lurked in the day ahead, and he felt the need to prepare himself. But when Maggie slid soapy arms around him and scrubbed his back, his tension ebbed as his desire rose. Beneath the waterfall he kissed her, wishing with all his heart that time would stop so they might stay right there forever.

Wrapped in a towel, he pulled the drape from the easel on which Maggie's portrait faced the north light. It had been her idea to include the old rocking horse. He was particularly pleased with the hand and arm that draped gracefully across the saddle as she sat in half-profile beside it on the floor. The bare feet were right, too, and typically Maggie. Her russet hair deserved to be featured, enhanced by ocher and olive; thus her peasant blouse and skirt had changed colors three times. Even now he wasn't completely satisfied. Was there too much umber in the curl that framed her face? Too little viridian where the hem of her skirt touched her calf? He had declared it finished nearly three weeks ago, had forced himself to concentrate on other projects. Yet doubt nagged at him. Is this what Clarke wanted? Would it please Maggie's mother?

Maggie thought it was perfect. So certain was she of its success, so lavish in her praise, that her step-father had waived his right of preview. He would see it for the first time this evening when Alex made the presentation.

He realized that his butterflies had as much to do with meeting Maggie's parents as with their reception of the portrait. But again Maggie had been positive.

"How could they possibly dislike you?" she asked reasonably. "You're handsome, educated, and enormously talented. What more could anyone ask?" She snapped him with her towel. "Now put your clothes on before you tempt me to do something wicked, and let's figure out how to gift wrap this canvas."

* * *

The sun sank behind the hills as the old Morris rattled north toward Dunany with Maggie at the wheel. That she loved to drive it was as amusing to Alex as it was puzzling. Why a girl with a Jaguar, a Bentley, and a Land Rover at her disposal would prefer his ancient vehicle with its bald tires and rusted fenders was beyond his comprehension. Now that he thought about it, there was much about Maggie he didn't understand, but perhaps it was better not to try. It was enough that she took pride in his work, that she laughed with him and ruffled his hair, that she shared her thoughts, her joy, and her body with him. Maggie loved him, he was sure, and beyond that nothing else mattered.

She rolled down her window and signaled a left hand turn to a lorry following behind.

"We can't be there yet," said Alex. "Dunany must be at least another twenty miles."

She swung onto a small, dirt road, avoiding pot holes filled with the morning's rain, and pulled over onto a grassy bank. Alex, though curious, knew better than to question her. Maggie would explain when she was good and ready.

"This will do." She turned to face him and took his hand, intertwining their fingers. "I want this to be a perfect evening," she began, "as perfect as the morning was."

"Of course. So do I."

"But it can't be perfect for me until I have been completely honest with you, told you something I probably should have said first off."

"Jesus, it must be serious. Let me guess—you're a vampire."

"Don't be daft. No, it has to do with the portrait."

"You've changed your mind about it?"

Maggie touched his mouth with her finger. "Of course not. Now, hear me out—please." She drew a deep breath. "Remember the day Derek and his girlfriend followed you and me to Killiney? I tried to get you to talk about your work, but you were so unnerved by your interview with Uncle Liam that you kept changing the subject."

"Uncle Liam?

"Oh, not really. He's just a good friend of Julian's who's known me nearly all my life. Well, I was so attracted to you that after we dropped off Derek's girl, I made him take me back to the Thane gallery so I could see what kind of a painter you were. Derek sometimes behaves like a dilettante, but he really knows art. Both of us were excited by what we saw."

"And?"

"And this is the hard part." She bit her lower lip. "I sensed that Uncle Liam's assistant was less than enthusiastic about your work. Clearly, he was campaigning for some Swiss landscape artist to be featured in their fall exhibit. So Derek and I recruited a few of our friends to visit Uncle Liam's Gallery—to pose as connoisseurs and rave about your work." She watched him warily. "It wasn't all a pose though. Two of them actually bought paintings."

" 'The Kirk of Corey' " said Alex evenly.

"No, that one's mine," said Maggie. "It's hanging above the mantle in my bedroom. I was afraid you might see it tonight and misunderstand."

Alex could not prevent bitterness from flavoring his voice. "So my big break wasn't due to talent after all—merely politics." He leaned back against the headrest and closed his eyes.

"I won't allow you to think that way!" she said firmly. "You can be angry with me if you like, but you must accept that ultimately your work earned its own reward. All Derek and I did was make some noise. That's just sound marketing, Alexander. Lights under bushels make poor beacons."

"And this commission by your step-father?"

"Strictly business," she said, raising her right hand. "Uncle Liam knew nothing about our little ploy when he recommended you to Julian. He still doesn't, for that matter."

Alexander watched the last of the sunglow turn the sky from cadmium to cobalt violet. He suddenly felt alien in Ireland with its searing passions and chilling stoicism. He missed the gentle, southern cadences of his homeland, the mosses, and the marshlands. At heart he was a Georgia boy who had been away too long.

"I'm glad at least of that," he said.

A few miles beyond Dunany, Maggie steered the Mini between twin gateposts and followed a long driveway around a hill through dense foliage. It culminated in a circle before a stately stone house whose wide steps were flanked by gas torches. Maggie parked the Mini next to Derek's Jaguar and gave Alexander a reassuring smile.

At the open door, a heavyset old woman in an apron scowled into the darkness. Maggie hugged her, laughing.

"Oh Marie, how I've missed your smiling face! Meet my American friend, Alexander Wade. Alex, this is Marie Toomey, Derek's and my old nanny. I haven't seen her since I left England last spring. Isn't she beautiful?"

"Behave y'self, Miss, or I'll be turnin' you over my knee." She eyed Alexander. "He's a tall un, ent he."

"And here's Julian!" cried Maggie. She ran into her stepfather's arms. "When did you and Mummy arrive?"

"Late this morning." He held her at arm's length. "Let me look at you. Something's different."

"Not something, Julian, everything! Come! Meet Alexander."

The two men shook hands solemnly, taking measure of each other.

"A pleasure," said Alexander.

"My daughter assures me we have a treat in store." He led the way to the grand parlor where a fire crackled on the hearth. Derek rose and held out his hand.

"So," he said, "we meet again." His handsome face, tanned from tennis, was thinner than Alex remembered, his frame more angular. Alex tried to picture Sam and Derek together, but the image wouldn't take shape.

Mrs. Clarke's face held promise of the woman Maggie would become. They shared hair and skin tones, identical straight noses, wide-set eyes. But Grace Clarke's eyes were blue instead of green. She smiled warmly at Alex and offered him a glass of sherry.

"Have you been in Ireland long, Alexander?"

"About four years," he replied, "although it seems longer. I haven't been home to the United States since Christmas three years ago."

"Your family must miss you terribly."

"My aunt, who took me in when my parents died, isn't very well—according to my sister, Charlotte. I feel torn between staying here where my work is and going home to be with Aunt Olivia in Georgia."

"Julian and I visited your Georgia about ten years ago. While he was involved in business meetings, I explored Atlanta. We hired a car for a day and drove about the countryside. It's lovely."

"Yes, and so is Savannah, but very different because of the ocean nearby. It's low country—marshland."

"One mustn't lose touch with one's home," she said softly. "Perhaps you'll spend Christmas in Savannah again this year."

When a manservant announced dinner, Alex held Grace Clarke's chair, then sat at her right as she indicated. Despite the opulence of the setting—tapestried walls, candled sconces, crystal and old silver—the family's open affection for one another put him at ease. From time to time throughout the meal he glanced at Maggie's face. She was radiant, her color high, clearly enjoying the electricity sparked by conversation among people she loved. She preferred to remain on the periphery, a quiet observer of friendships in the making. He felt honored by her love, and something else — committed. I will never let her be hurt, he vowed, never let her down.

A silver coffee service was placed before Grace Clarke as they settled themselves again before the fire. She filled a delicate demitasse with espresso and handed it to Alexander.

"When may I have the privilege of seeing some of your work?" she asked.

He glanced at Julian, who gave a slight nod. "Mrs. Clarke, it will be my pleasure any time. Perhaps you'll excuse me for just a moment."

He pulled the portrait from the back seat of the Morris and carried it up the steps into the foyer where Maggie waited, her eyes dancing with excitement, her finger to her lips.

"How many years, my love?" they heard Julian ask.

"Ah, Julian, twenty wonderful years. Here's to the next twenty." Their cups clinked.

"And now for the pièce de resistance!" he said, sweeping his hand toward the doorway where Maggie waited with ill-concealed delight.

"Ta daa," she laughed.

Alex leaned the portrait against a winged chair opposite Grace, and together he and Maggie removed the wrapping. All three of the observers gasped in unison as the last of the paper fell away. For a long moment, nobody spoke. Then Grace began to cry quietly, her hands over her face.

Derek was the first to recover himself. "You have to understand, Alex, that my mother has always been a bit daft. She laughs when she is upset and cries when she is happy."

He leaned forward to get a closer look. "This portrait is a wonder — the ultimate magic. You've taken a toad and made her into a princess!" He glanced sideways at his sister, who stuck out her tongue.

"Oh, Alex," said Grace rising to deliver damp kisses, first to Julian, then to him. "It's magnificent! You've captured the real Maggie — my Maggie. I can't remember when I've been so undone." She began to weep again.

Maggie hugged him, her eyes shining. "You see? I told you!"

"My boy, I can't tell you how delighted I am, although not surprised considering your endorsements by both Thane and Arthur Dowd. But portraits are emotional, highly personal things. It's rare to find one so honest, so totally — right. I'm sure there are many creditable artists who can reproduce lines and colors accurately. But you've gone well beyond that. You have somehow managed to capture Maggie's spark — a moment of her animation — where her real beauty lies. No easy task." He clapped a paternal hand on Alex's shoulder. "Well done, my boy. I have a feeling we're going to be hearing a good deal about Alexander Wade from now on."

"Thank you, sir. I'm very glad you're pleased."

Until that moment Alexander had given little thought to the fact that his sessions with Maggie were over. In the last couple of months, he had come to regard her as much a part of his studio as his easel or his palette. She ornamented his dreary flat with her presence, lending color and, yes, animation to an otherwise drab existence. What would happen to their closeness now that the portrait was finished? Could he perhaps persuade her to sit for him again?

An hour later any momentary doubts he had were

dispelled as she walked him to his car. A procession of clouds paid court to the three-quarter moon riding low on the horizon. Maggie, humming softly to herself, imprisoned his hand on her hip as she matched his stride.

"Do you think I'm beautiful?" she asked.

"Of course I do. Why do you ask?"

"To make you say so," she smiled. "And do you love me?"

"I love you." He gave her hand a squeeze.

"And when you go home to Georgia, will you take me along?"

"If you like."

"Good!" she said, pulling him close. "I shall go right in and tell Mummy and Julian I'll be spending Christmas in America."

"But—"

"Now don't you dare say anything to spoil it. By then your show will be over, and you will have been proclaimed 'foremost young artist of the decade.' Everyone will be ringing you up with offers of commissions, invitations to galas, introductions to her majesty the queen—just think how tiresome!" Her laugh rippled out across the night. "Seriously, Alexander, doesn't your Aunt Olivia deserve to share a little in your triumph? Like a small return on her investment?"

"You make it all sound so simple and inevitable."

"I have never been more positive of anything in my life. When will you learn to trust my judgment?" She pulled his face to hers and kissed him fiercely. "Now go home. I want to stay here tonight to be with Mummy and Julian. But I'll ring you in the morning and, if it's a nice day, perhaps we'll drive south along the River Barrow to Waterford. There's an old mill there where one can buy the best soda bread in Ireland."

All the way home an idea was taking shape in Alexander's mind. If Maggie were right and the show did shift his career into forward gear, he need not stay in Ireland. Both Thane and Dowd had expressed confidence in his work, had promised him exposure. Now with Julian Clarke as a powerful ally, his celebrity would almost certainly extend to England and France as well. He could paint damn near anywhere he chose. The thought so liberated him that he goosed the Mini up an incline and tore through the moonlight down the other side. No more leaking ceilings and recalcitrant radiators. He would go home to Savannah, by God, and he'd take Maggie with him. Tim would be glad to forward his mail. But just in case plans changed at the last minute, he wouldn't alert Auntie O. in advance. He could just imagine the look on her face when he and Maggie burst through the front door of Hibiscus House with their arms full of packages.

*T*omochichi made a ritual of licking his forepaw and swiping it across his face to remove the last traces of milk from his whiskers. Then he sprang onto Alexander's old desk and curled around himself, his tail across his nose. A noisy purr advertised his contentment.

"You're lying on my list, you useless old thing," said Olivia affectionately. She scratched him under the chin, remembering his unpromising arrival at Hibiscus House thirteen years before. She and Lucy were listening to the weather report and packing away Christmas tree ornaments in the same green cardboard box the family had used for twenty years. A hard freeze had just been predicted when they heard someone thud through the back door and clatter down to the kitchen whistling "Dixie" off key. The two women exchanged an amused look. Alexander was home, his shirttail flapping, his Christmas sweater a wad in the crook of his arm.

As he gently placed the mound of blue wool on the kitchen table, his whistle diminished to a whisper. Within the sweater's soft folds, a wet, grey creature lay still as death.

Lucy recoiled in disgust. "Don't you be bringing no dead rat into this kitchen!"

But when the kitten struggled to lift its head and issued forth a pathetic mew, she muttered off to the pantry to fetch some dry towels. Alexander stayed up all night keeping watch and gentling warm milk onto its tiny tongue with a medicine dropper.

Shortly after dawn when Olivia crept downstairs to start the teakettle, she found Alexander sprawled in Lucy's old rocker like an abandoned marionette, but the pathetic creature had vanished. In its place sat a fluffy kitten calmly appraising them and currying a white forepaw. By the time Alexander, sticky-eyed with fatigue, stumbled off to bed, Tomochichi had secured a home, a name, and a friend forever.

"Why must you always be the center of attention?" asked Olivia. She ignored his baleful look and extricated her note pad from under his haunch. "Crossword puzzles," she read aloud. "Embroidery. Chess." Not a very impressive list. There must be something else she could do. She tried to remember what her life was like when Carter was alive. She had always been so busy then, but doing what?

Well, gardening for one thing. She had spent hours dusting, fertilizing, and pruning her roses in the shade of late afternoon, and her Lady Anns were the envy of all her friends. She smiled remembering how each morning she had clipped a new bud for Carter's lapel. How wonderful he had looked in his pin-striped suit, his watch fob draped across his vest. He always kissed her cheek with a look of surprise as if she hadn't given him a rosebud every spring morning of their married life! She gazed out the window at the dogwood tree, its few remaining leaves tinged with red in the early evening light. It looked so hopeful—all budded up for next spring despite its bare limbs.

"Green thumb," she wrote.

Fresh flowers always cheered her up. She had a sudden vision of herself arranging daisies in a low silver bowl. Her fingers, nimble then and graceful, had trimmed and poked and shaped with confidence, creating a fragrant centerpiece for her dinner table. She had loved the contrast of her delicate Limoges plates against ivory damask, delighted in the sparkle of crystal and silverware in candlelight. Everyone said she was a superb hostess, and Olivia knew it was true. She had a talent for pairing guests, for pleasing palates, and for drawing people out. Always shy as a girl, she was amazed to feel so comfortable entertaining Carter's business associates and their wives. She enjoyed planning menus and designing seating arrangements, tendering invitations, and recording pleased acceptances. She liked watching Lucy in command of her kitchen, sampling sauces and issuing instructions to temporary help. But most of all she enjoyed the look of pride on Carter's face—in his wife, his home, and himself.

"Good listener," wrote Olivia with satisfaction.

And what else? She looked about Alexander's room for clues. If she held very still, she might catch the echo of his arrival after school, his lunch box banging against the stair wall. No matter how tidy he looked when she sent him off in the morning, by four o'clock his knees would be muddied, his shoelaces dragging. Lucy would hustle him off to wash his face and hands before she gave him cookies and milk.

"Pralines," she wrote.

She wondered if he still dropped books and caromed off door jambs. It was a marvel that a boy who couldn't begin to hit a baseball could put a jigsaw puzzle together in a flash. How beautiful his earnest child's face was when he concentrated, how deft his little hands. She had sometimes wept watching him sleep, loving him so. Her sister-in-law Abby's death had broken her heart, but the gift of her son had mended it. All Olivia wanted in the world was for Alexander to be happy.

"Model ships," she added to the list.

She thought about the poster paints she had given him their first Christmas together. Five small jars of color — red, yellow, blue, black, and white — lined up in a hinged wooden box. Beside them was a groove for a brush and a tin cup for water. So vivid were the colors, so pristine, that it was New Year's Day before he could bring himself to unscrew the lids. For weeks they had worked together creating on shelf paper chapter after chapter of the adventures of Captain Chance, a pirate with a pet cobra. She watched his mouth work in concert with his steady hand as he labored to prevent the colors from flowing into one another, to keep the brush rinsed between dips. In the spring when the paints were nearly gone, he began to experiment with mixing colors, intrigued by the varieties of hue within his power. Another box of paints followed the first, and then another. At fourteen Alexander took a job walking Lou Ainsworth's cocker spaniel and invested all his earnings in linseed oil, gesso, turpentine, and tubes of pigment.

Olivia worried that so solitary a life was not healthy for a growing boy and urged him into high school sports. So he went out for the track team and spent even more solitary hours jogging around Forsyth Park to build up his endurance. Out of loyalty, she attended most of the meets.

"Don't be an old fool," she said aloud, erasing

"cheerleader" from her list. Tom yawned and rolled onto his back, inviting a belly scratch.

She caught herself whistling under her breath as a tune threaded through her mind. What was that ditty? Something about automobiles. Olivia smiled recalling how the three of them would sing at the old upright after dinner. She knew a hundred songs in those days when she and Alexander sat side by side on the piano bench with Carter behind happily bellowing, "She's only a bird in a gil-l-l-l-ded cage . . ." in his lusty baritone, his hand over his heart.

She saw herself in the red-sequined dress bought when she was twenty to fill in for Melody Lange at the Rainbow Club in Brunswick. Night after night the audience had joined her uncertain contralto in a repertoire of music hall songs; seldom would they let her go without two or three encores. Except for having to fib to Papa, she had been happier in those three weeks than she had ever been, and until she fell in love with Carter a year later, she seriously considered pursuing the life of a performer. When Elizabeth Gaylord discovered Olivia's secret, she was horrified to think her daughter would even consider such a "tawdry" occupation. At her mother's insistence, Olivia promised to keep the truth of her unseemly behavior from her future husband—and so she did for the rest of his life.

Now, however, she tossed her pencil aside and hurried up the dusty stairs to the attic. Somewhere amid all the discarded Parcheesi boards and dressmakers forms and boxes of books—ah, yes. Uncle Morton's old steamer trunk. She found a screwdriver and pried upward on the corroded latch. A little puff of dust billowed forth as it gave way, causing her to sneeze.

On top lay a tissue-wrapped lace dress that Olivia

didn't recall packing away with the rest of Abby's things. She lifted it from the trunk and carried it to the tiny window for a better look. How Carter had admired his beautiful sister in this dress, one that Olivia coveted but was never able to wear. At Abigail's urging she had tried it on once, but the champagne color was all wrong, making her skin look sallow and her hair dull. Olivia sighed, remembering how gracefully Abby's neck had risen from the deep vee of the bodice, how beautifully her dark curls cascaded down her back. The swan and the ugly duckling. Yet jealousy had never interfered. More like sisters than sisters-in-law, they had also been best friends.

"Someday I will marry a tall, handsome man with a moustache, and he will adore me," Abby had stated firmly. "And when our son and daughter are grown, we'll travel abroad every summer — to the Alhambra or the Pyramids or the Taj Mahal. And I will absolutely die before I let myself get old and fat like Mrs. Donner next door."

It was remarkable to consider how closely Abby had predicted the course of her own life. Before their marriage, Weston Wade's elegant good looks appeared often beside a variety of southern beauties in the society section of the *Savannah News Press*. Until, that is, he danced one dance with Abigail Thornheart at the Telfair Ball. Olivia watched all spring with fascination as her sister-in-law, like an expert fisherman, enticed him with the lure. By June he was hooked, and they held a Christmas wedding.

Because of the difficulty of Charlotte's birth, Abby began to doubt she would ever have the son she planned. But her patience was rewarded when, with neither problems nor fanfare, little Alexander arrived eight years later to make the family complete.

Her dreams of travel, however, never came true, for one April afternoon when the children were nine and one, Abby discovered a lump in her breast. Two years later she was laid to rest in Bonaventure Cemetery.

Olivia carefully returned the dress to its tissue and searched deeper within the trunk, lifting out a military uniform of Carter's, a smoking jacket with velvet lapels, a pair of embroidered slippers for feet much smaller than her own, and, tucked down in one corner, a cloth-covered diary faintly scented with jasmine. The brownish ink on the inside cover was difficult to read in the dim light, but Olivia recognized it immediately. For a moment she sat staring at the signature, listening to the thud of her heart.

The writing was as familiar as her own—round and feminine. She could picture Abby's slender hand holding the fountain pen, could see her mouth set in concentration as she bent over the page, her mahogany hair fanning over her shoulders like a shawl. She would pause in thought, nibbling at her lower lip, then continue slowly, sensitive to the appearance of the page.

They kept few secrets from each other, eager to heighten the delights of youth by sharing. Often they exchanged little treasures to celebrate their sisterhood — Abby's cloisonné pill box, Olivia's long braid — indulging themselves in poignancy and the sweet pain of sacrifice.

But here in Olivia's hand was the greatest gift possible, a treasure made all the more precious by its journey down through time. When she had packed it away after Abby's death, Olivia was too grief-stricken to read it. Now, for reasons she couldn't explain, the moment seemed right. Resisting the urge to read randomly, she determined that tonight in bed she would start at the beginning and savor every word.

Slipping the little book into the pocket of her dress, she dug deeper in the trunk until finally, at the bottom, her fingers identified the prize she sought. With a little cry of pleasure, she withdrew a flat box fastened with a tired rubber band that disintegrated at her touch. Olivia held her breath and lifted off the lid. The sequins had faded a bit, but the scarlet dress still shimmered in the dim light. She hurried downstairs and inspected it closely in her sunny bedroom. Would it still fit? With a giggle of naughtiness, she shrugged out of her cotton dress and pulled the slinky fabric over her head, taking care not to catch it on her hairpins. As the heavy skirt shimmered to the floor, the years vanished, and Olivia was once again the young chanteuse whose nimble fingers flew effortlessly across the piano keys.

She ignored the side zipper that would no longer close and, lifting her skirt, descended the stairs to the parlor. Her hand trembled slightly as she lit the candelabra atop the piano. Then, with a deep breath, she slid onto the bench and lifted the lid, exposing yellowed keys.

Tentatively at first, she picked out the melody with one finger, smiling as it began to come back to her. Stiffened fingers worked awkwardly as she fumbled for the left-hand chords, and she winced whenever she hit a wrong note. But after a couple of tries, she gathered speed and confidence. The third time through, Olivia began to sing.

> My daddy drives a Packard
> My mama drives a Ford
> My lover drives a Chevrolet
> But I don't drive, oh Lord, oh Lord
> I don't drive, oh Lord.

Delighted with herself, Olivia swung into to a rendition of "Sweetheart of Sigma Chi," then "Tea for Two." This was fun. She had forgotten how much she enjoyed making music with her own hands. Maybe if she practiced a little each day, she could relearn some carols in the few weeks remaining before Christmas. Then when it was time to donate her annual holiday ham to Azalealand Nursing Home, she could also bring a little music into the patients' lives! Perhaps Dr. Bluhm was right — she did have something to offer others. Oh, if only Alexander could come home for the holidays. A good old-fashioned, noisy Christmas would set her right again. She ran her thumb up the keys in a jubilant glissando.

Then she sighed. Just today a letter had come from Ireland full of excitement about his show in Dublin next week, but he hadn't even said he missed her — let alone mentioned coming home.

Olivia tried to remember if Alexander had ever had a girlfriend. Not a steady one, she decided, although at her urging he did take Pastor Wrenn's daughter Penny out a few times.

"I never know what to say to girls," he had complained. "They've all seen different movies and read different books than I have. All they want to talk about is clothes and parties and who's going with who."

"Whom, dear."

"Whom. I don't understand why I can't just stay home with you and Tom and Lucy."

"Because, darling, part of growing up is learning to make conversation with all sorts of people. It's important to your future that you establish friendships. Being close to others helps keep a balanced perspective on things, don't you see? But in order to *have* a good friend, you must first learn to *be* one."

Good advice, thought Olivia. She wondered why she didn't follow it herself. A balanced perspective was exactly what she lacked if Dr. Bluhm's analysis was correct. She studied her reflection in the gilt mirror over the mantle. Am I getting senile? she wondered. How is one to know? She couldn't count on friends to tell her, so concerned were they for her feelings.

The only unbalanced person she had ever known was Carter's Uncle Morton who lost his hearing at sixty. For years the family blamed deafness for his conversations with himself, but gradually it had become apparent that Uncle Morton "heard voices." Over the years his monologue became more and more animated, his behavior increasingly bizarre, until finally he had to be cared for in a nursing home. The last time she had seen him he hadn't recognized her. His eyes wild, he had spent the duration of her visit arguing incoherently with an invisible roommate. Poor Uncle Morton had died of a stroke while confined to a bed with sides. Horrible!

Olivia rose and drew close to the hall mirror, searching her face for signs. Is craziness visible? She looked the same as always, or did she? Was that a twitch in her right eyelid? And what caused those dark circles? It's true she hadn't been sleeping well, but perhaps that, too, was a sign of a disturbed psyche. She remembered how Carter's family always made excuses for Morton's strange behavior, always pretended it was perfectly normal to sit at the dinner table mumbling and gesticulating. Was she being patronized like that by Dr. Bluhm? By Beau Harris? By Lucy?

"What nonsense!" she scolded herself. She shimmied out of the red dress, pulled on an old cardigan from the front hall closet, and went down to the kitchen to make herself a sandwich.

The news was just starting as she flicked on the little TV on the kitchen counter. She rummaged in the pantry for a plate and a new jar of mayonnaise, then took lettuce and leftover turkey from the refrigerator. She was still a little annoyed at Lucy for insisting on making her a real Thanksgiving dinner. How on earth would she ever eat all this? She'd have to freeze at least five pounds of it.

The weather forecast promised a fifty per cent chance of rain. Good, thought Olivia. The garden could use a good soaking. She spread margarine on one side of her bread and mayonnaise on the other. Then she began slicing down through the breast, sharing the scraps with Tomochichi and glancing occasionally at the tiny screen. So much ugliness in the world, she thought. It seemed as if everyone was stealing from, lying to, or assaulting everybody else. What happened to the easy, gentle days of the 1950's when the stock market was healthy and peace allowed mothers and wives to sleep at night? Wasn't there ever any happy news to report? If her hands had not been so greasy, she'd have snapped the TV off.

"And now on the local scene," said the newscaster, "it seems another ghost has made its appearance in Savannah's Victorian district."

Startled, Olivia lost her grip on the knife and sliced down hard on her left hand. Blood immediately began to pump from her lacerated palm. The shock of it made her lightheaded and, for a moment, she didn't know what to do. Then, wrapping it tightly in a dish towel, she dialed Lucy's number and listened to it ring twice—three times—while holding her injured hand aloft. On the fourth ring, Jonas picked up.

"Thank heaven you're home," said Olivia. "Is your car working? Could you, perhaps, run me over to Candler Hospital's emergency room? I've made a rather bad slice in my hand, and I think it's going to need stitches."

"Lord, Miz Livvy, let me pull on my shoes. I'll be right there."

Olivia kept pressure on her bleeding hand as she watched the TV camera pan a run-down neighborhood, then focus in on a three-story frame. It was Lucy's house! But in all the confusion of the last few minutes, she had missed the details. The story was just concluding.

"Subsequent to these events," said the reporter, "Mr. and Mrs. Smally declined to be interviewed on camera. I'm Sylvia Sloan for WSAV News."

Olivia scooped up Tomochichi with her good hand and kissed him on the top of his head. "Well, old chum," she said with a chuckle, "If I'm a nutcase, at least I'm not the only one!"

* * *

Two hours later she was home again, sporting an ace bandage over the surgical dressing on her left hand. She struggled into her nightgown, then tingling with anticipation, turned back the covers on her canopied bed.

As she pulled Abigail's diary from its hiding place, a heavy vellum envelope slipped from the middle pages and fell to the floor. It was embossed with the name "Chatham Diagnostic Center" and addressed to Mrs. Weston W. Wade. Abby had slit the top with her ivory letter opener, careful not to create ragged edges. Holding her breath in anticipation,

Olivia withdrew the letter inside and unfolded it. The typeface looked old-fashioned even to her unpracticed eye. She adjusted her reading glasses, leaned toward the light, and read:

May 23, 1975

Dear Mrs. Wade:

After assessing your daughter's test results and completing the requisite interviews and observations, Drs. Sternberg and Gregory concur with my diagnosis of sociopathic dysfunction. All agree that intensive psychotherapy is indicated for proper management of Charlotte's condition — preferably, as I suggested to you in our conference, at a residence facility such as Forest Park or St. Boniface.

With your permission, I shall draft a report to both institutions immediately to set the wheels in motion for her admission — assuming there are openings. If not, we can explore other options. Given the serious nature and increasing frequency of her destructive behavior, especially where the baby is concerned, I hope you can persuade Mr. Wade to support you in this effort. I can not emphasize strongly enough the urgency of immediate intervention.

Please communicate your wishes to me at the earliest so that we may proceed with appropriate treatment.

Yours truly,

Arnold Wells, M.D.

Olivia forced herself to breathe; her fingertips tingled, and she felt lightheaded as if she might faint. Apparently, Carter had hit the mark about Charlotte when he called her "a changling with a twisted psyche." Chaotic images tumbled around in her mind: Alexander's bruises and unexplained infant screams; Charlotte's sudden weight loss; the look of tight-lipped tension on Abby's face whenever the subject of psychiatry was raised.

Olivia's face flamed as she remembered the only serious disagreement she and Abby had ever had—the time Olivia dared to suggest that Charlotte's behavior was unnatural for a child of five. She would never forget her sister-in-law's stricken look.

"You know it was an accident," Abby had cried, "just an unfortunate accident. How can you even suggest a little girl would deliberately do such a terrible thing!"

"Because," Olivia had replied, "I made a point of telling her what a skull and crossbones means and why I was locking the bottle away in the medicine cabinet. I deliberately waited until she went downstairs to hide the key in my jewelry box, but when we were all having lunch in the garden, she found it and unlocked the cabinet by standing on the sink. She emptied the whole bottle into the fish bowl, Abigail. I found her standing perfectly still, so intent upon the death scene that she didn't hear me call her name." Olivia didn't add that this incident was not the first—that it followed a series of wingless butterflies and one-legged crickets.

Abby's response was to retreat into silence and withdraw from Olivia, who thus learned her lesson well: Never again did she interfere in the Wade's family life.

"Sociopathic dysfunction," she whispered. But even if Charlotte's father had continued to resist, why didn't Abby persevere? Surely she recognized that Charlotte needed help. She looked again at the envelope; the postmark explained everything. Six months after May 23, 1975, Abigail Wade was dead.

A sudden chill gripped Olivia. She zipped the letter into the inner pocket of her purse and hurried back to bed.

* * *

Lucy had always found the mailman's name amusing. That Mr. Post enjoyed his work was evident by his brisk walk and sharply pressed uniform. He took pride in knowing everyone on his route by name and made a point of inquiring about the health of new babies and oldsters.

"Morning, Lucy. How's Mrs. Thornheart doing?"

"She got herself a headache this morning. But on the whole she pretty good, thanks, Mr. Post. What you got for us today?"

"Nothing very interesting. Some bills, I suspect, and a registered letter for Mrs. Thornheart from some probate judge. Tell you what—you just sign her name right here." He handed her a pen. "Any more offers on your house?"

"Not since our haint made the news." She cackled and slapped her thigh. "But we sure got us a steady parade of lookers! Lordy, they just set out front in them cars and stare at our front door like we was gonna jump out and say 'Boo!' I swear, we beginning to feel like goldfish." She gave him a little wave and shut the door.

Lucy stood in the foyer and glowered at the letter from the office of Honorable Judge Byron F. Denny. She didn't rightly know just why, but for some reason it felt like trouble. For a moment she was tempted to open it but quickly changed her mind, knowing Miz Livvy would have a conniption. She laid the bills in plain sight on the hall table, then reluctantly placed the other envelope on top, uttering a silent prayer that the old lady would be strong enough to handle whatever evil was inside.

E ven if the program had been fascinating, the chink of silverware and rattle of plates being served would have made it difficult for Charlotte to hear from table number fifteen. In addition, two of the young matrons at table sixteen were exchanging gossip in a monotone just loud enough to be heard but not overheard. She was sure she caught Mindy Moore saying "Farley," but she couldn't get the next few words. She studied Mindy's profile, trying in vain to lip-read.

She glanced around the room at the other Junior Leaguers, all of whom seemed engrossed in the speaker's polemic against the proliferation of advertising along Interstate Highway 16.

Charlotte had had an altogether awful morning. First, her maid cancelled. Then, Aunt Olivia called and tried to cop out of this afternoon's session with Dillman. It had taken a good twenty minutes and a heavy guilt trip to convince the old ninny not to bail. And now here Charlotte sat pretending to enjoy rubbery chicken and canned peas while enduring the discomfort of having her consciousness raised. Billboards, she thought in disgust. Give me a break.

She thought about the half pack of Marlboros that had lain in the drawer of her bed table since December 31. Even a stale cigarette would taste wonderful just now. But last New Year's Day in a moment of weakness she had made two mistakes: She had made a bet with Farley that she could quit smoking, and later that afternoon, after three — okay, five — mimosas, she had agreed to accompany her sister-in-law, Debra, to Manfred Dillman's C.B.E. group the following week. That was when she first heard his theory of neuroses being the mind's way of defending against "excessive psychobiologic pain." Dr. Dillman had explained that to be gratified, "such needs must be owned, felt, experienced," and he instructed the group participants to "look into the mirror of their infancy and see themselves literally reaching out for the comfort of human touch when hungry, discontented, or afraid." By the end of the session all the members — except for Charlotte — had come to experience what Dillman termed "the Catharsis of Basal Embrace," a release from "the separation of one's self from one's primal feelings," a purging brought about by hugging — and being hugged by — another human being. What a load of bullshit.

Despite Debra's urging, Charlotte had not been persuaded to attend another session — until three days ago when it occurred to her how potentially useful Manfred Dillman might be. Debra was delighted when her sister-in-law called to make arrangements for herself and Aunt Olivia.

Charlotte smiled at her table mates and rose, holding one finger at her lips. As unobtrusively as possible, she threaded her way between tables to the ladies' room, where she unzipped her purse and withdrew her little silver flask and the computer copy she had hurriedly printed out that morning. The article discussed poisonous house plants, poisonous ornamentals, poisonous trees and shrubs.

She studied the symptoms caused by the first three plants on the list, all of which could be found in the garden behind Hibiscus House. "Oleander: Extremely poisonous leaves," she read. "Affects the heart, produces severe digestive upset, and has caused death." But not always, thought Charlotte, bringing the flask to her lips. She read on. "Foxglove: Large quantities of leaves cause dangerously irregular heartbeat and pulse, digestive upset, and mental confusion. May be fatal." Who would forgodsake notice if Olivia suddenly exhibited mental confusion? She laughed to herself, enjoying the vodka's bite. But again, death was not certain. "Wisteria: Seeds and pods cause mild to severe digestive upset." No mention of death.

Disappointed, she started to fold the paper back into her purse, when "Mistletoe" caught her eye. "Fatal," she read. "Both children and adults have died from eating the berries." Perfect! She couldn't remember a single childhood Christmas when Uncle Carter hadn't hung mistletoe above several doorways, demanding kisses from all who passed beneath. If Aunt Olivia was not out of Hibiscus House by Christmas, Charlotte vowed to revive this old family tradition. She lifted the last of the vodka in a silent toast to better days ahead.

* * *

At a few minutes before three, Charlotte, Olivia, and Debra joined several others on the elevator to Dr. Dillman's fourth floor office. Punctuality was paramount, for their hour-and-a-half session could not begin until all were present. Charlotte knew Arnie Stoddard would have arrived early to make the coffee and help set the chairs in a circle. She decided to choose a seat as far away from him as possible, disgusted by the possibility that she might have to endure his blubbery embrace, her cheek crushed against his sweat-dampened shirtfront. It was tricky to avoid both Arnie *and* Myra Vernon, who sucked rhythmically on her ill-fitting dentures.

Recognizing Arnie's green sport coat on the back of one folding chair, Charlotte chose three seats on the opposite side of the circle. She could not bring herself to call Dr. Dillman "Freddy" as he preferred. Yet to address him as "Dr. Dillman" implied a respect for the man that she didn't feel and couldn't fake, so she avoided the problem by refusing to call him anything at all.

At precisely three o'clock, Freddy arrived, beaming as always. He greeted each member with a show of warmth, inquiring about their week and offering hugs to all. Charlotte offered her hand and quickly introduced Olivia, toward whom he turned the full force of his charm, insisting that she sit by his side as an honored guest. Then he cleared his throat importantly.

"We have with us today," he began, summoning the deepest bass possible. His stentorian delivery always reminded Charlotte of church, making her wonder why, since he liked to pontificate, he hadn't chosen the ministry instead of psychology. Maybe, she thought, because he couldn't see over the top of the pulpit.

"We have a guest with us today, one who has enjoyed a long, full life in Savannah, brought to us by her loving niece, Charlotte Horner. Someone please offer a hug of kinship to

Mrs. Olivia Thornheart." Leaping to her feet, Nadine held out her arms to Olivia, who flushed at finding herself the center of so much attention.

"Thank you, Nadine. Now as I'm sure you recall, at our last meeting," said Freddy, consulting his notes, "Carl shared some of his concerns about his relationship with his father. We encouraged him to purge and promised him the comfort of our arms. Because the session lasted somewhat longer than planned, we didn't have time to hear from Myra. But she has graciously consented to begin our meeting today." He paused for dramatic effect. "So, if you're comfortable, my friends, let us begin. Myra?"

"Well," she said, sucking at her teeth. "I seen how you all helped Carl. But I don't rightly know that you can do anything for me."

Freddy encouraged her with a smile. "What seems to be the trouble?"

"Well, me and Harry, we only got one son—that's Jeffrey—and now he's gone off and got married and Harry says 'thank God' and I feel like I'm gonna die or something. Seems like since Jeff's been gone, I can't hardly drag myself out of the bed in the morning I'm so weak. I don't eat right, I don't sleep at night, and that isn't all." She turned her wedding band round and round her finger. "I keep having dreams like I'm at my own funeral, only it isn't me laying there—just somebody pretending to be me. Harry, he don't even listen." The frequency of the sucking increased. "The last time I told him I think I'm gonna die soon, you know what he does? He gets up out of his chair and goes to the kitchen and picks up one of the two chops we was gonna have for supper and slaps it back in the freezer. 'Ain't no use wasting good food,' says Harry, and goes back to reading his paper." She started to cry, her alternate sniffing and sucking making her words nearly unintelligible.

Arnie passed Myra the tissue box, and Joan poured her a glass of water from a carafe on a side table. Several group members took turns putting their arms around Myra, patting her shoulder, and offering words of comfort.

Freddy waited until Myra's hiccupping subsided.

"What do you think is the cause of your extreme fatigue?" he asked gently.

"I don't rightly know. Except there don't seem to be no reason to get up in the morning. It seems like Jeffy, he don't need me now he's got him a wife. And Harry, he don't even know I'm there unless his stomach growls. And sometimes I just feel like it don't matter if I'm dead or not 'cause nobody'd notice anyhow."

"We'd notice," said Carl. He reached over and took her hand. "The group wouldn't be the same without you."

She sucked her teeth loudly, then gave him a watery smile, her mascara leaking into the creases of her cheeks.

"Let us show you by our actions, Myra, just how important you are to us," said Freddy. "Please rise and accept our love."

Myra, a beatified look upon her thin face, stepped to the center of the circle. First Freddy, then Debra, then Carl, then Wendy, Nadine, and Joan offered her their embrace. Both Charlotte and Olivia remained firmly in their chairs.

Settled again, Freddy turned to Olivia.

"Mrs. Thornheart, you've seen how our little group works together to ease each other's psychic anguish. Perhaps you'd care to share with us one of your own concerns. Please, Olivia (we're all on a first-name basis here), make us a gift of your pain so that we may introduce you to the catharsis of basal embrace." Brace, race, ace. His melodious basso ricocheted around the room.

"Oh my goodness," said Olivia, "I hardly think I— Oh, dear me."

"Don't be nervous. We are all frightened children sometimes. Each of us needs to reach out to another human, to feel the reassurance of our mother's arms enfolding us as we experience our space." His voice grew even deeper. "Let us *be* there for you, Olivia. Share your angst with us, and accept from us your reward."

"Oh but I . . ." said Olivia, glancing nervously around at the expectant faces. "I don't really know what to say."

"Just tell us what's on your mind."

"Well, I don't really have any angst to share, only the smallest concern because I'm having trouble sleeping, and even that . . ." Her voice faltered.

"You don't know how lucky you are!" wailed Myra.

"Hush now, dear, it's Olivia's turn. You were saying?"

"Charlotte thinks I need to get out and socialize more. That's really why I let her talk me into—why I agreed to come here today. Because both she and Dr. Bluhm seem to feel I spend too much time alone and need to expand my outside interests. But I had no idea that this was—that I would be asked to—"

Freddy's voice deepened confidentially. "Are you lonely, Olivia?"

"Not especially," she said, plucking at her skirt. "My friend Lucy comes every day, and her son Jonas is around from time to time. And of course there's Charlotte." She sent a tremulous smile in the direction of her niece.

"Do you like living alone?" intoned Dillman, furrowing his forehead with the appearance of concern.

"Oh yes. But you see, I'm not really alone. My cat, Tomochichi, keeps me company. And for the last couple of months, whenever I go to bed—"

"Don't be a bloody fool!" boomed Cyrus.

"Whenever you go to bed—" prompted Freddy.

"Where have you been!" demanded Olivia. "I haven't heard from you for at least two weeks!"

Arnie's jaw dropped. Carl and Maria stared bug-eyed, first at each other, then at Charlotte who seemed to have been transported elsewhere. Myra's dentures grew silent.

"You know I can't manifest without your help!" Cyrus exclaimed. "Doubting me as you have been doing causes all my essences to enervate. This is the first time you have acknowledged my existence in over a fortnight!"

"Why, we've all been sitting right here, Olivia, giving you our fullest attention," soothed Freddy.

"Oh dear me," said Olivia, glancing around at the circle of concerned faces. "I do apologize."

"And so you should," grumbled Cyrus.

"No apologies necessary," said Freddy. He turned to the group. "Shall we show Olivia she is no longer alone? Shall we help her to experience her first cathartic awakening? Please step forward, friend, and open your heart to our embrace."

Awash in sympathy, Myra led the way. She gave Olivia a peck on the cheek, and, with an extra squeeze, released her into Freddy's waiting arms.

ucy crammed her Sunday hat on her head and grabbed her straw tote from the knob of the broom closet. She slammed and locked her back door, then stomped through the parlor toward the front hall. Jonas' tool belt lay in her path, and she sent it smashing against the wall with a vicious kick. Then, remembering, she hurried upstairs to her bedroom to fetch the note she had written to herself. Where was it? From a pile of papers on her dresser she pulled a scratch pad and, without a second glance, crumpled the top sheet into a ball and stuffed it savagely into her pocket. Nobody — not nobody — was gonna get away with this!

Lucy locked the front door behind her and pounded down the walk to Jonas' Chevy. On top of everything else, they would probably be late. Just let those white folks say one word to her about it! She'd really enjoy the chance to rip 'em up one side and down the other.

When the old car shuddered to a stop in front of Hibiscus House, Jonas jumped out to help Olivia into the back seat next to Lucy. He tried to catch her eye with a smile, but she just looked flustered and a little vague. He steered the sagging Chevy around as many bumps as possible, studiously avoiding his mother's evil-eyed expression in the rear-view mirror.

"You wait right here!" she snapped, as he pulled over and opened the rear door for them. "Don't you be going to The Rail for no beer!"

She slammed the door hard enough to knock Jonas' glasses askew. He hadn't seen her so steamed since that August day two years ago when old lady Washington's electricity had been cut off in the middle of a 100° heat wave. Mama had sure looked militant as she marched into the Broughton Street offices of Savannah Electric. For a little, bitty woman, she sure could raise some sand! Jonas maneuvered the Chevy into a metered parking spot across from the courthouse and settled down for a doze.

As Lucy followed Olivia up the steps and through the heavy glass doors, some of her passion dissipated. Clearly this was enemy territory, and the fact that Miz Livvy had been ordered to appear made Lucy feel like a criminal. She flattened out the crumpled paper from her pocket and reread it for directions. Two o'clock, fifth floor, Courtroom 5C.

The only other time she had gone to court was when Mr. Bates was arrested at 3 a.m. for sleeping on a bench down on River Street. The police had thrown him in the drunk tank, and it took a lot of talking to convince them he was just wrung out from the night shift sweeping up at Barnaby's after working three twelve-hour days on Captain Crowne's trawler. Lucy knew all about drunk tanks and vagrancy charges, but a competency hearing was something else again. She clutched the lapels of her coat tightly together at her throat and steered Miz Livvy through a heavy oak door at the end of a long hall.

The courtroom was not at all as she remembered but looked much larger with only a few people present. And while Perry Mason's cases had always been tried in oak-paneled stateliness, Chatham County's beige painted walls made her feel like a child in school again. At the foot of the center aisle stood a tall man with a briefcase. He greeted Miz Livvy and ushered her to a seat at one of two tables in front of the judge's bench. Lucy supposed he was the junior partner from Olson, Quinn, and Farwell substituting for Miz Livvy's longtime friend and counselor, Charlie Quinn, who was recovering from a heart attack. She studied the young man, trying to assess whether he knew what he was about, and decided he looked more like he was in costume for the senior class play than like a real courtroom lawyer.

At the other table sat Charlotte with her father-in-law, Harold Horner, and behind them sat a short man with a moustache and a thin, sallow woman who rocked silently back and forth, sucking her teeth. The four talked quietly among themselves, occasionally glancing over in Olivia's direction.

Lucy settled herself on a hard wooden bench near the back and removed her coat. Lordy, how she did sweat when she was nervous!

* * *

At 1:59 two men whom Olivia didn't recognize—one short and one tall—entered through the double doors at the back and strode down the aisle to join Charlotte and company. Simultaneously, the judge emerged from his chambers and took his place behind the bench. He arranged a file of documents before him, switched on a tape recorder at his elbow, and, with a glance around at the expectant faces, began.

"Good afternoon, ladies and gentlemen. I'm Judge Byron F. Denny, on the bench today to hear the petition before this Probate Court brought by Mrs. Farley Horner and her co-petitioner, Mr. Harold Horner, concerning the alleged incapacitation of Mrs. Olivia Thornheart. Is Mrs. Horner present? Ah, yes, and Mr. Horner? Good. And Mr. Frawley, you are counsel for the petitioner, right?

"Now, Mrs. Thornheart, we want you to relax and feel comfortable about asking any questions or voicing any concerns you may have regarding these proceedings." He glanced at Mr. Tims, her young attorney, assessing his readiness, then smiled reassuringly at Olivia. "Is there anything you'd like to say before we begin?"

"Yes," said Olivia, perching on the edge of her chair. "Of what am I accused, exactly?"

Judge Denny smiled. "This isn't a trial, Mrs. Thornheart. You aren't accused of anything. You have expressed some concern to your friends and your physician about your health — your mental health — and that concern is shared by your family. We are here simply to bring an objective view to the matter in an attempt to determine how best you may be helped."

"My family? You mean my niece, Charlotte Horner."

"Yes, and Mr. Harold Horner, specifically."

Olivia squirmed in her hard wooden seat. "I beg your pardon, Judge Denny, but by no stretch of the imagination is Harold Horner 'family.' I fail to see what possible benefit to him could accrue from investigating my 'mental health.'"

"None whatsoever, Mrs. Thornheart. It is the benefit to

you with which we are concerned here. You seem agitated. Is there something else on your mind?"

A warning signal flashed in her mind. She must get hold of herself, contain her frustration, her fear. She must weigh every word carefully so as not to be misconstrued. But she felt such rage! How dare Charlotte subject her to this humiliation? Even if I *am* a bit forgetful, she thought to herself, to whom am I a danger? Olivia cleared her throat.

"Will you be good enough to explain, please, how you came to know of my personal concerns—since I am told all information exchanged between doctor and patient is privileged?"

"Indeed it is, Mrs. Thornheart. This court has no specific knowledge, merely general information imparted by you to various people in this room." He gestured toward the table where Charlotte sat impassively among her supporters. Of the four faces, only Myra Vernon's bore evidence of tension. Her blue eyes darted from Judge Denny to Olivia to Charlotte and back to the judge again. Clearly anxious, she nibbled at her already mutilated fingernails.

"I see," said Olivia. She allowed herself to slump a little to ease the small pain forming in her abdomen.

"Now perhaps you'll be good enough to answer a few questions for us." Judge Denny shuffled through some papers in front of him and adjusted his reading glasses. He peered across the top of them at Olivia, who fixed her eyes on an emergency exit sign and avoided his gaze.

"Are you still suffering from insomnia?"

Olivia felt trapped. If she said "no," she'd be lying—something she'd never been able to do with any success. Even if she managed to keep her voice natural, her face would flame, and red blotches would blossom on her neck, giving herself away to the most casual observer. She flashed on her child self telling her mother she had been to choir practice when in reality she had spent the hour playing jacks in the park with the Kimble brothers. With one glance at her face, Elizabeth Gaylord had dispatched her daughter to bed without supper.

On the other hand, if she answered "yes," she might help them build a case against her.

"Mrs. Thornheart?"

"It's true that I have recently had some difficulty sleeping."

"And for this reason, you asked your physician for sleeping tablets?"

"Yes."

"That was the only reason?"

"Yes." What an absurd question, she thought. Why else would I want sleeping pills?

Judge Denny consulted his paperwork. "And he recommended alternative remedies?"

"Yes." She wondered why he persisted in asking questions to which he clearly knew the answers.

"Do you have any thoughts on why you continue to lose sleep?"

"Dr. Bluhm thinks—"

"*Your* thoughts, Mrs. Thornheart."

"Judge Denny, I'm seventy-nine years old. It's my understanding that this stage of life is often characterized by sleeplessness. We exert ourselves less; as a result, we need fewer hours of rest. I dare say when you're seventy-nine you'll have trouble, too." She tried to smile in order to lend her statement an air of confidence, but her lower lip felt paralyzed for some reason and her cheeks weren't working right. A twitchy little grimace was all she could manage. "I have come to view insomnia as just one of the many penalties for an overlong life."

"Do you feel you have lived — overlong?"

"Not especially. I still enjoy my home, my friends."

"Ah, yes. Your home. It suffered fire damage some time back, is that not true?"

"Yes." Olivia was glad his attention to her sleeping habits had been diverted.

"But you were not injured."

"That's correct."

"You were in the house?"

"I was asleep on the second floor."

Judge Denny thumbed through the file of papers before him and, found the one he sought, and paused to read. "How did the fire start?" he asked finally.

"A lighted candle apparently ignited some papers in the wastebasket."

Judge Denny removed his glasses and chewed thoughtfully on the temple as he glanced again at the report before him. When he spoke, his voice was gentle, as if cushioning the effect of his words. "Did you perhaps drop that candle into the waste basket, Mrs. Thornheart?"

Olivia gasped. "No I did not!" She looked frantically for support from her attorney, but he was busy scribbling notes on a yellow pad. At the other table Charlotte and Harold sat in whispered conversation. Only Dr. Dillman and Myra seemed to be listening.

"Do you enjoy alcoholic beverages, Mrs. Thornheart?"

"On occasion," said Olivia, her heart pounding.

"On *that* occasion?"

"Yes, I did have a cocktail that evening. It had been an especially trying day, and I—"

"Just one?" Judge Denny narrowed his eyes. "Let's be accurate on this point. Didn't you, in fact, have several?" His fingers drummed impatiently on the desk.

"Your Honor, isn't this line of questioning a bit—" began Olivia's young lawyer.

"You'll have your opportunity shortly, Mr. Tims," interrupted the judge. "Now then, Mrs. Thornheart, isn't it possible that in your quite diminished state, you saw a way to end your own 'overlong' life by setting Hibiscus House on fire?"

"It is not!" The pain in Olivia's stomach stabbed sharply. "I merely forgot to lock the back door, and someone walked in and started the fire while I was asleep." How could he even suggest such an awful thing!

"Do you have trouble remembering things—like locking your door at night?"

"My housekeeper calls to remind me." Olivia swiveled in her chair to search for Lucy's reassuring presence. For the first time she admitted to herself how dependent she was upon that phone call and felt the fabric of her self-confidence rapidly unraveling.

Again the judge paused to review his notes; then he uncapped a black marking pen and wrote something on a pad at his elbow. The scritching sound set Olivia's teeth on edge, and she realized she was holding her breath.

At last Judge Denny leaned back in his chair. "I notice you are wearing a bandage on your hand, Mrs. Thornheart. I trust you are not currently in any pain."

Olivia noted the friendly tone that had returned to his voice. Her anxiety abated a little, and she settled more comfortably in her chair. "Not any more. I'm to have my stitches removed on Wednesday."

"An accident?"

"Yes. I was watching the news and slicing turkey. Something startled me, and my knife slipped. It was quite a nasty gash." Good grief, was it possible he was suggesting she had deliberately hurt herself?

"Do you recall what startled you?"

Olivia fidgeted in her chair. Silence ballooned as Judge Denny let the question hang in the air.

"They reported a haunting in a nearby neighborhood on the six o'clock news." She made a quick survey of faces, but all remained impassive. She felt herself relax a little.

"Does that frighten you?"

"Frighten me?" She chuckled. "Not at all. I don't believe ghosts are motivated by malevolence."

Judge Denny hesitated, choosing his words carefully. "I saw the same news story. The reporter seemed to think the ghost was deliberately trying to dissuade a couple from buying the house."

"He was. That is—" Olivia's fingers fumbled with her gloves.

"How do you know?"

"I'm—just supposing."

The judge cleared his throat and clasped his hands in front of him. "Since you have introduced the subject," he began, "perhaps you'll share with me some of your own experiences concerning ghosts."

Olivia sat in stunned silence. She now realized the reason for the presence of Dr. Freddie Dillman and Myra Vernon at Charlotte's elbow. How could she have allowed herself to be manipulated into revealing her relationship with Cyrus in front of Charlotte's C.B.E. group! And Harold! He was no doubt itching to tell the court all about her one-sided conversation in Bonaventure Cemetery. She was relieved to see her banker, Beau Harris, sitting a few rows back. At least she had one friend in court. Or did she? Hadn't Beau made it quite clear that day in his office that he thought her irrational for attempting to buy Lucy's house? Was that what all this was about? Her money? How had this happened? Her head spun and the pain churned upward toward her heart.

"Oh," she moaned. "Oh, dear. I do feel quite ill." She blotted her mouth with a handkerchief.

Furious, Lucy sprang from her seat at the back of the courtroom and hurried to Olivia's side. Although she had never once laid a hand on Miss Charlotte during her childhood, it took every ounce of her willpower not to do so now.

Judge Denny compared his wristwatch with the clock on the wall overhead. "I will adjourn this hearing until three-thirty in order that Mrs. Thornheart may have a bit of a rest." He gathered his papers together and without further comment disappeared through a door behind his leather chair.

At the direction of Mr. Tims, Lucy bundled Olivia onto a couch in the fifth floor library and pulled off her shoes. "Don't you move, Miz Livvy. I'm gonna find you an aspirin and a glass of water. I'll be right back."

At the sound of the door closing, Olivia sat up, frantically searching for an escape route. The window, she knew, was not an option; Montgomery Street was five stories below. The only door led to the corridor from where muffled voices could be heard. She was trapped here without anyone she could trust to advise her. These people were trying to persecute her, to distort even the most innocent things in order to make her appear unbalanced and a danger to herself.

Suddenly, a great weariness suffused her, and she sank back down in exhaustion. Let them do it, she thought. Let them ask all the questions they want. She had neither strength to resist nor confidence in her sanity. Lulled by a roaring in her ears, she flung a heavy arm across her eyes.

"Bloody bastards!" fumed Cyrus.

"Go away."

"You mustn't capitulate, Olivia. Didn't I tell you that wicked tart was up to no good? Wasn't I right when I said she's been plotting against us all along to appropriate my house and turn it into a bloody hostelry?" The room suddenly felt stifling.

Olivia clamped her hands over her ears and squeezed her eyes shut. "I can't listen to you anymore. I mustn't say another word."

"This is no time to be fainthearted! Brace up, and into the breach! Together we'll devise a plan. No greedy little baggage is going to prevent me from fulfilling my promise to Meg. Dear God in heaven, what wouldn't I give to evanesce right this very moment!"

* * *

At 3:15 Olivia marched through the courtroom door and down the center aisle. She planted her feet firmly in front of Mr. Tims and squared her shoulders.

"Be good enough to inform Judge Denny that I have refreshed myself and wish to meet with him privately before we proceed with this appalling charade," she snapped, riveting the startled young man with her eyes. "And tell him to be quick about it because I bloody well have more important things to do!"

Three minutes later she was ushered into chambers and offered a seat in the leather wing chair across from Judge Denny's desk. She perched on the edge, clutching her purse firmly, a determined set to her jaw.

"I hope you're feeling better, Mrs. Thornheart," said the judge with a sympathetic smile.

"Indeed I am," said Olivia, her eyes never leaving his face. "Not only am I feeling better, I'm also thinking more clearly."

Judge Denny made a tepee of his fingers and leaned slightly forward on his elbows. Without his robe he looked much less threatening, rather like Mr. Fargo, the plumber. He returned her gaze and waited politely.

"Your honor, one of the most difficult things about growing old is learning to accept change with grace." Olivia turned her wedding band around and around behind the swollen knuckle. "Children of my generation were taught to treat our elders with courtesy and to listen respectfully to what they had to say — not because they were such admirable people but because each of their many years had added to their storehouse of experiences, both good and bad, from which we could learn. My family, though neither wealthy nor perfect by any means, had a strong sense of pride. We considered it very poor taste to air our dirty laundry before strangers, so to speak.

"Today —" She looked up from her lap and shook her head. "I tremble to think what my mother would say about a niece parading an intensely private family issue before public scrutiny!"

"My dear Mrs. Thornheart, please be reassured that

while the proceedings of this hearing do become a matter of public record, there is little likelihood that they will interest anyone beyond those directly involved."

"Nonetheless, I find the whole matter appallingly tasteless. However!" Olivia stood up abruptly and straightened her spine. "Times change, your honor. For reasons of her own, Charlotte Horner has opened Pandora's box, and there's no turning back." Olivia unzipped the inner pocket of her purse and extracted a yellowed envelope. "Before we resume this wretched inquisition, there are a few things about your 'petitioner' I think you need to know." Without further comment, she handed over the letter containing Charlotte's psychiatric evaluation.

*J*onas shifted his tool box to his left hand and felt around in the jumble of his pocket for his house keys. The boss wanted the cottage on Harris Street ready for drywall before the Christmas break, and that would mean long hours for the next two weeks. After today's ten-hour shift, all he could think of was kicking off his shoes and popping open a beer. He hoped Aunt Sis had fixed supper, but he'd bet next Friday's paycheck that she was upstairs in his old room watching TV.

He shouldered open the front door and dropped his tool belt amid the jumble of boots, umbrellas, and cans boxed for recycling. Sure enough, no cooking smells wafted from the kitchen. And when he called upstairs, Aunt Sis didn't answer. Jonas tossed his keys on the mail table and flung himself face up on the sofa, vowing to rise again in just ten minutes.

Poor Mama. For the second Friday in a row she had set out early going from one rental property to another trying to find a suitable house or apartment big enough to accommodate the three of them but cheap enough to afford.

Jonas wondered where they would all be living one year from today. Not too long ago a lot of landlords couldn't hardly keep their spaces rented. Only poor folks was willing to live in the rundown apartments available in this part of town. Then Savannah got "discovered" thanks to some Yankee who wrote a book about it and made it famous. Next the sailing Olympics happened right out there beyond Wassau Sound. And sure enough, pretty soon rents began to rise. Jonas loosened his laces and toed off his work boots with a sigh of relief. The last thing he had wanted to do was move back into his Mama's house, but his dinky little fourth-floor walk-up had gone from $350 to $500 a month—more than his paycheck could handle.

When the front door opened thirty minutes later, Jonas was in the kitchen frying sausages in the black iron skillet. He was surprised to hear Aunt Sis' voice arguing with Mama.

"Seven blocks from the bus stop! How'm I supposed to get me to the doctor?"

"Nothing wrong with you that some exercise wouldn't cure," retorted Lucy. "We all gonna have to make concessions."

"How'd it go?" Jonas asked.

Lucy washed her hands at the kitchen sink, then tied an apron around her waist. "Well, we looked at four or five places, but only one looked likely. Smaller than this, but a nice big kitchen. Got a little patchy yard out back."

"Where?"

"Over east on Juniper Street." She sighed. "Transferring twice gonna make it more'n a hour bus ride to Miz Livvy's house on days you can't drive me."

"Juniper Street—that's way over in Thunderbolt!"

"*Way* over. Makes my feet hurt just thinking about it, " grumbled Aunt Sis.

"How many bedrooms?"

Lucy sank onto a kitchen chair with a sigh. "Two."

"Two! Mama, how we going to make do with two bedrooms?"

"Well, I figure me and Sis can share the big bedroom in front, and you can have the smaller back bedroom. It'll work." She sighed again. "It'll have to."

Jonas understood his mother's discouragement. To her, moving out of this house was an occasion for mourning, like burying an old friend. He cast about for a way to cheer her up.

"Tell me about the kitchen," he said, relieved to see her brighten.

"It's almost as big as this, only it's got more cupboards. And guess what — a dishwasher! Can you imagine? Even Miz Livvy don't have a dishwasher! Needs cleaning and a coat of paint. And two of the windows panes is broken." She set about peeling potatoes. "No gangs though," she said. "Told them I'd be back on Monday to sign a lease. I got to put up two months' rent."

"Lotta money for just two bedrooms," said Sis.

"You got a better suggestion?" challenged Lucy.

When the doorbell rang, Lucy handed Jonas the potato peeler and hurried out of the kitchen. A moment later she returned, her eyes wide, her face strained.

"Make some coffee," she said to Aunt Sis. "That real estate lady from Franklin and Hay is in the parlor wantin' to talk to me about something."

"Guess we didn't find Juniper Street a moment too

soon," sighed Aunt Sis. Shaking her head from side to side, she began measuring coffee into the strainer.

Quietly Jonas closed the kitchen door behind his mother. "How is it—really?" he asked.

"Pitiful," said Sis. "Roaches everywhere, and the yard ain't nothing but a bunch of broken glass and rubble. Lucy kiddin' herself about no gangs. The house next door got 'Sultans' and 'Demons' and cuss words spray painted all over the side." She looked at him and shook her head. "First thing we got to do is get a new hot water heater. Old one all rusted out."

"How much rent?" asked Jonas.

"Six-fifty."

Jonas seized the fork and poked savagely at the sausages. "We ain't *never* going to be able to come up with six-hundred and fifty dollars every month. She must have lost her mind!"

"Don't let your mama hear you talking like that," said Aunt Sis. She grabbed a sauce pan out of the dish drainer and slammed it onto the stove.

"Talk like what?" Lucy reappeared in the kitchen door and stood studying them both, her hands on her hips. Finally she sighed. "I guess it's time you heard something I never told you before. Sit down, boy," she ordered. Jonas sat.

Lucy regarded him a moment longer, then began circling the kitchen table, hugging herself with her arms.

"Once when you was about twelve, your daddy lost his job," she said, frowning at her son. "We was living on the second floor of your grandpa's house over near Garden City—real crowded too, only three bedrooms for the six of us. The winter was hard, and there wasn't much construction goin' on in the city, so your daddy and your uncle Ben was laid off. Just about that time, Grampa Bates had a stroke and had to go to the hospital. He got better, but it took a long time, and all of us was picking up whatever extra jobs we could find to help with expenses. There wasn't never enough money, though, and we got further and further in debt.

"One night your daddy came home real tired and discouraged. He said he never wanted to eat no more beans and went straight to bed. At least I thought he went to bed. But I never seen him so beat down before — he was always a smilin' man, your daddy — so I went in to see if I could cheer him up." Lucy stopped pacing and stood staring out the kitchen window at the evening sky.

"He was sitting there in the dark, and I don't think he even knew I was in the room at first. It scared me so bad, I didn't say anything. When I finally reached out to take his hand, he jumped like somebody punched him. That's when I felt the gun." Lucy's eyes closed momentarily; then she began to pace.

"He says to me, 'I used to have such hope.' I remember clear as day that he gave this kind of laugh that really wasn't no laugh at all, just a mournful little bark like a wounded dog. He says, 'You and me, Lucy, we was gonna to have our own farm. We was gonna get us a house and grow onions and thank God for clean, rich dirt.'" Lucy fought for control of her voice. "'But I don't even think about that no more. It ain't never gonna happen, so what's the use?' He was really meaning to shoot hisself, too, I know it. I took his hand with the gun and lifted it to my own head. 'Then let me be first,' I says. For a minute he didn't make a sound. Then his big shoulders started to shake. I put my arms around him and rocked him back and forth like he was a chile until he got it all cried out. Afterwards I wrapped that gun in my apron and ran all the way to the river and threw it out into the water far as I could." She turned to her son. "The next week Captain Crowne gave your daddy a job painting one of his trawlers." She ran her sleeve across her tired eyes. "Don't you ever let me hear you say 'never' no matter how hard life gets. You owe that much to your daddy."

Lucy plunked down on a kitchen chair and pointed a finger at Jonas. "Now you get down on your knees, boy."

"Aw, hell, Mama."

"Do as I say, Jonas. You get down on your knees and fetch that bottle of whiskey in the back corner of the kettle cupboard. Sis, you get us three of them fancy little glasses on the top shelf over there next to the sink. We got us some serious celebrating to do!

"What about?" asked Jonas, handing her the bottle.

She measured out three shots of whiskey, then raised her glass on high. "Here's to hope!" she laughed. "Here's to haints. And here's to hell with Juniper Street!"

Sis stared at her sister-in-law as if she'd lost her mind. "Lucy Bates, what on earth you talking about?"

"I'm talking about that nice Miss Hagin from the real estate office who came all the way over here just to bring me the good news. It seems that television report about us having a haint in the house made folks sit up and take notice. The folks at the Historic Savannah Foundation heard about all them out-of-state cars stopping out front and persuaded the folks who own this building not to sell it for condominimums but to leave us just the way we is—except we gonna be historically *restored* and *preserved*, praise God." She cackled at the look of amazement on their faces and tossed off her whiskey in one gulp. "The real estate folks is coming tomorrow morning to take down the sign." She slammed down her glass and reached for the bottle. "It'll be at least a year—maybe two—before we got to look for another place. Now y'all go ahead and tell me what you have to say about that!

*T*he maitre d' bowed slightly and swept his hand toward a table near the fountain. "Just here," he said, pulling out a chair. Charlotte slipped into place and accepted a menu. "Would you care for an apéritif?"

She wiggled the toes of her right foot to restore the circulation, aware of a tenderness already developing on the back of her left heel. It had been a mistake to wear her new pumps, but she had wanted to look her best for this lunch date at Chez Nous, and they matched the patent leather purse and her black linen suit. She crossed her legs, enjoying the whisper of new pantyhose, and tugged slightly at the slim skirt that barely reached her knee. Yes, black was definitely her color.

"Double vodka on the rocks," she said.

The maitre d' bowed again and disappeared taking with him the card that said "reserved."

Charlotte looked across the top of the yellow rose in its bud vase to the center of the courtyard where water spouted from the panpipes of a dancing faun. It cascaded down mossy rocks and spilled into a circular pool inhabited by black and orange koi. Baroque music seemed to follow its descent. The effect was theatrical ("cornball" Farley would say), but she liked it—a little bit of glamour to liven up this one-horse town.

She watched a couple being seated at a table to her left—in their sixties, she decided. He settled the rosy, laughing woman in her chair and snugged her sweater around her shoulders with an affectionate squeeze. Then with a scrape of his own wrought-iron chair, the man sat across from her, beaming his pleasure. Neither one wore rings.

Could they be lovers? Charlotte wondered. She studied them with clinical interest, noticing how even at their advanced age they managed to observe human mating rituals—leaning toward each other as they spoke, touching each others' hands. Charlotte shuddered, imagining them in bed together—sagging flesh, varicose veins—and instinctively straightened her spine and tensed her abdomen.

She tilted the face of her newly repaired watch toward a shaft of sunlight. Mary Finn was already ten minutes late. Her eyes swept the small crowd of people gathered at the reservation desk and sighed with impatience.

The maître d' whisked back and forth across the courtyard ushering people to their tables and issuing muted orders to the busboys. With a starched napkin, he swept imaginary crumbs from a nearby chair, then helped an elderly woman to be seated. Charlotte wedged off her left shoe and probed the spongy back of her heel with her finger. It felt hot and tender. Damn, she thought with rush of irritation.

When a waiter set a glass on a doily before her, she

sipped and checked her watch once again. Twelve-forty-five. Ten minutes more—then she was out of here. Mary Finn could forgodsake buy her own lunch.

Evidently the elderly woman was lunching alone, for the waiter had removed the second place setting from her small glass table. He set before her a dessert plate and a cup of coffee. Will that be me? Charlotte wondered. When I'm eighty, will I put on a hat with wilted cloth flowers and take myself out for dessert? Will I pretend to be waiting for someone to join me, even though Farley and all my friends are senile or bedridden or dead?

She watched the old lady take a tiny bite of what looked like fruitcake, then dab daintily at her lips with her napkin. What useless creatures old people are, she thought. Like Aunt Olivia—merely taking up space in a world to which she contributes nothing! She drummed her nails on the table in irritation, then glanced again at her watch. At eighty, she thought, I'll probably still be sitting here waiting for Mary Finn.

Suddenly inspiration struck like a jolt of adrenaline. Of course, fruitcake! All old ladies loved the stuff. As long as Charlotte could remember, Aunt Olivia had served one of those disgusting Claxton fruitcakes to drop-in guests at Christmas. With all that lumpy, rum-soaked fruit, who would notice the addition of a few little white mistletoe berries?

She had pushed back her chair and collected her purse when she saw her friend making her way across the room. "I was just leaving," she said.

"I'm so sorry," panted Mary Finn, slipping into the opposite chair. She smoothed her hair and signaled for the waiter. "Forgive me."

"Only if you tell me you're late because you sold the Bates house."

"I wish," said Mary Finn, grimly. "Perrier with lemon," she said to the waiter.

"So the fat people with the poodle declined?"

"Apparently Savannah totally spooked them — so much that they've taken their Peoria house off the market." She sighed. "Not only that, Mel Franklin just canceled the listing." She gave a wry smile. "Not one of my better days."

"You mean the Bates house is no longer for sale?"

"Nope. In light of its recent notoriety as a 'house of spirits,' the place has become one of the favorites of the tour bus crowd. Anyway, the owners are applying for a low-interest loan through Historic Savannah Foundation to fund restoration of the house. Retaining it as an historic single-family residence will make it worth a lot more when the neighborhood revives — as it's certain to do. In the meantime, they'll file for a homestead exemption, which will give them a tax break." She shook her head. "For them it's a win-win situation."

"What am I going to forgodsake do?" said Charlotte.

"You! What about me? This is my livelihood we're talking about. Do you realize I haven't sold a single property in nearly two months?" She glared at Charlotte, whose attention was upon the fountain in the center of the courtyard, her chin in her hand.

The waiter appeared with his pencil poised, affording the two women a few moments' distraction. When he left, Charlotte blotted her mouth on her napkin. "You're right," she said. "It's your *career* that's at stake. Whereas it's only *my life!*"

"Don't be a drama queen."

"You just don't get it, do you. You don't see that my entire future rests upon gaining title to Hibiscus House and making it into a successful business venture. It's really all I have that's mine."

"Stop whining, Charlotte," snapped Mary Finn. "It's unbecoming in one so privileged." She counted off on the fingers of her left hand. "You have a good education, a successful husband, a lovely home, a new car, and a closet full of designer clothes. And some day you and your brother *will* gain title to Hibiscus House. In the meantime, can't you think of something more constructive to do besides harassing that old woman? Get a job. Join a gym. Volunteer at Candler Hospital. But for Christ's sake, leave your Aunt Olivia the hell alone!" She stood abruptly and threw her napkin beside her plate. "Please cancel my lunch order. I've just remembered there's someplace else I need to be."

*T*he flying saucer thrust free of Earth's gravitational pull and spiraled toward the heavens. Higher than the faces of staring children, past the nests of squirrels, beyond spheres of mistletoe caught in the treetops it soared, exposing its underside to Earthbound spectators. As it rose, it picked up speed, then leveled off on a trajectory toward Atlanta. Just when it seemed certain to disappear among the clouds, the silver disk hesitated as if experiencing some terrible malfunction. For a moment it hovered above the upturned faces, then plunged Earthward in an erratic wobble. Listing more and more, the saucer crashed to the pavement and rolled on edge to a stop on top of Olivia's foot.

"'Scuse," panted a boy in muddy shoes as, in one graceful movement, he bent to retrieve the frisbee from beneath her bench and arc it skyward again.

Olivia sat quite still feeling acutely, not for the first time, the essential malevolence of the world. Take, for instance, Forsyth Park. Once its azalea-bordered walkways and stone benches had afforded a quiet sanctuary for nannies with carriages, for ladies in flowered hats to take a bit of air and exercise. Now derelicts claimed the benches, urinating in the bushes and littering the grounds with their styrofoam cups and cigarette butts.

Recalling the genteel pleasure of chamber music concerts in the park, Olivia shrank from the jungle sounds blaring in stereo from the boom box nearby. It wasn't their music that offended her, nor the boisterous fun of the young people enjoying their game. It was their total dominance — visually and aurally — of all that was public, their aggressive disregard for the values, preferences, and privacy of others.

She sighed. So precarious was the issue of safety these days that most older citizens felt they could no longer venture forth in the cool of evening as they once did to enjoy the company of neighbors around the square. Just last Monday old Colonel Quick had been assaulted by hoodlums in his Whitaker Arms apartment and hospitalized with multiple lacerations and a fractured jaw. He could purchase another TV, but the vandalized portraits of his dead wife and children were irreplaceable.

Even one's own family harbored unsuspected dangers. Despite the fact that Judge Denny had decided in Olivia's favor the issue of her mental competence, Charlotte's defeat in court left Olivia feeling more vulnerable than ever. How did it go, that poem by William Congreve so often quoted by Carter?

"Heaven has no rage like love to hatred turned,
Nor hell a fury like a woman scorned."

She had never understood her niece's psyche, but through experience she had come to expect duplicity. There was no doubt Charlotte would seek revenge if she ever found out Olivia had shown her psychological evaluation to Judge Denny. The only uncertainty concerned the form her niece's fury would assume. The threat of such unbridled malice stalked Olivia's dreams.

Yet what other choice could she have made? Her niece had declared war, and in order to defend herself, she had followed the only course of action open to her. Although sharing Charlotte's history with Judge Denny had not resolved the issues of the competency hearing, Olivia knew it caused him to view his "petitioner" in a new light—the edge she needed to prove she was as competent as anybody else.

Discovering that her foot had fallen asleep, she rotated her ankle and flexed her toes until the tingling abated. Then leaving the screeches and thrums of the boom box to their gyrating audience, she limped to a quiet bench closer to the fountain near the north end of the park.

What had prompted this bizarre arrangement of spouting water fowl and mythical creatures, half-man/half-fish, she couldn't imagine. But they had performed their watery ballet in this place since 1858. It was gratifying to note that at least some things endured.

A child in pink, her beaded braids spiking from her tiny head, ran forward to get a closer look. She stood with thumb in mouth watching the afternoon sunlight dance among the spray. After a long moment, her exuberance burst forth in a high squeal as she flung her arms high and ran away among the trees. Now that, thought Olivia approvingly, was an entirely appropriate response to such mad whimsy as Forsyth Fountain.

Warm weather had lasted well into fall this year, and

even now in December the park was somewhat green. From this vantage point she could barely see Hibiscus House so thick was the foliage of the moss-draped trees. But she could clearly see the iron gate on which Alexander had once loved to swing. Did the sunlight make it look rusty like that, or was it sorely in need of a new coat of paint? There were other things that needed her attention too — like a Christmas wreath for the front door. But she had little heart for the project and even less energy. It all seemed so pointless — absurd really — for an old lady spending one more Christmas alone. Olivia closed her eyes, losing herself in the music of the fountain.

The blare of a horn drew her attention again to Hibiscus House where a yellow cab had paused illegally to discharge some passengers. She watched the driver lift the trunk lid and unload several items of luggage; then, after a few words with one of his passengers, he squeezed behind the wheel and sped south on Whitaker Street. She watched the woman help the man wedge several smaller parcels under each arm as he held the two heaviest suitcases. Then she picked up a smaller case and a box tied with twine, playfully giving her companion a kiss before stuffing one final package between his teeth. They looked so happy and young together, each muffled against the chill in matching plaid scarves. Even from this distance and without her glasses, she could see they were in love. Olivia smiled. It was impossible to stay gloomy when all around her was vitality and youth — however noisy young people might be. Something about the man's posture caught Olivia's eye as the young couple struggled with their packages — a familiar lift of one shoulder, a characteristic buckling of his knees as he threw back his head in laughter.

And suddenly Olivia was running, running — in quick, short steps across the expanse of sidewalk circling the fountain, past a startled squirrel who scuttled for shelter, through the last red gold of autumn—with her heart in her mouth.

"Whoop! Whoop!" was all she could manage as she plunged across Whitaker Street, amazing herself with her own speed. Her strangled sounds caused the man to turn, and his face split wide. With one great yelp of joy, he emptied his arms and caught the old lady, whirling her round and round like a mad dervish.

"Whoop!" cried Olivia once again and burst into tears.

"We'll have to get you some proper track shoes first thing in the morning," laughed Alexander. He held her at arm's length and mopped awkwardly at her face with his handkerchief. Then he grabbed her and hugged her again. "God, it's good to be home!"

Maggie stood apart smiling at their shared joy. Auntie O. had played a supporting role in so many tales of Alexander's boyhood escapades that she seemed familiar in all but face. So *this* was the one who had helped him with his sums and taught him songs in Pig Latin, who had slept in a chair beside his bed while he raged and thrashed with scarlet fever. Listening to stories of his childhood, Maggie had often wondered if Olivia Thornheart had any idea how deeply Alexander loved her. Seeing them together, she didn't wonder anymore.

Alexander took Maggie's hand and smiled into her eyes. "Was I right?" he asked. "Didn't I say she was wonderful?"

"Your nephew has quite forgotten his manners," she laughed, "but we must forgive him just this once. I'm Alex's friend, Maggie Bisby. Delighted to meet you at last."

Olivia's eyes danced. "You're more than a friend as I could plainly see from across the street." She gave Maggie a quick welcoming hug. "Oh, how wonderful! Not one but *two* surprise visitors! I can't wait to call Lucy!"

Dividing the load, they hurried up the front steps and into the warmth of Hibiscus House.

Thirty minutes later Lucy stood frowning at the spot on Alexander's cheek where she had just planted a kiss.

"Don't they eat nothing over in Ireland? Lordy, look at them bones!" She poked a finger at his ribs through his sweater. "We'll fix that situation starting right now."

"What do you think of my girl?" Alexander pulled Maggie close.

"I think," retorted Lucy, "you better be marrying her right quick before somebody smarter'n you come along and snatch her away, that's what I think!" She cackled at the flush that rose in his face, then lumbered off toward the kitchen.

Olivia filled three sherry glasses.

"Pretend it's champagne because this is a real celebration. Why, only an hour ago I was sitting over in the park reminiscing about the times when we all lived together in this old house—you and Carter and I—wishing I could have those precious years back again. And all of a sudden here you are, like a wish come true."

They lingered over dinner enjoying Lucy's cheese soufflé, the intimacy of the gathering darkness, and each other's company. Olivia asked a thousand questions.

"Tell me about your show."

"It was quite good actually, if I do say so myself," said Alexander. "It enabled me to make some important contacts."

"Listen to this man!" exclaimed Maggie rolling her eyes. "It was *not* 'quite a good show,' it was a terrific success—a real coup—and you know it! On the last night after the word got around, there were so many people that the guards had to funnel them in twenty at a time every half hour. I used to think all Alexander's dissembling was false modesty, Mrs. Thornheart, but I've since concluded that he hasn't the least notion of how really talented he is."

"Can we trust your impartiality?"

Maggie laughed. "Perhaps not totally, but I heard Max Beale, one of the most respected curators in London, warning a dealer from Antwerp that if he didn't make his move soon, he'd be kicking himself a year from now! And Fulton Forbes from *Art World* wants to do a story while we're here."

"Have you any idea how long that will be?" Olivia hoped the question sounded casual.

"Well, certainly until after New Year's," Alexander replied, "and then we'll see." He smiled across the table at Maggie. "We have some decisions to make between now and then."

They took their coffee in front of the parlor fire. After the long flight and the excitement of the reunion, Maggie's eyes felt heavy. She snuggled close and rested her head on Alex's shoulder, her stockinged feet tucked beneath her. Despite all his reassurances, she had still felt anxious about meeting his family and feeling comfortable with their American ways. But she needn't have. Auntie O. was just as warm as he promised, and this wonderful old house reminded her of her family's winter home in Bordeaux. The ambience was the same: light and airy during the day; cozy and full of secrets at night when the shadows hovered in the corners. One could almost feel the presence of Thornhearts a hundred years gone.

Alexander kissed her solemnly at her bedroom door.

"Good night, sleepy head. I'll miss your cold feet, but I'm not sure how Auntie O. would feel about . . ."

"Hush," whispered Maggie, touching his lip with her fingertip. "I *want* to sleep by myself. I've much to think about, and having you next to me is a terrible distraction."

In his own room, Alexander sat on his old bed and looked around at the relics of his childhood — a tennis racquet, all the *Tarzan* books, a ukulele — and on the dresser a profile of his mother with a flower in her hair. Abigail Thornheart Wade was a beauty all her life until cancer cruelly withered her flesh and snatched away her curls. Though her face was lost to him, Alexander recalled the stroke of her hand on his hair as she bent over his bed. He remembered little else except part of a song she sang to him in a low, whispery voice:

> I'll build you a boat
> With a pretty white sail
> To cross the silvery sea.
> But you must promise
> Someday, love,
> To sail back home to me.

He knew Auntie O. had approved when he christened their model ship the *Abigail Ann*. But in his child's heart it had been more than a remembrance. The little schooner was like a promise to his mother not to forget — a sailing ship, as her song requested, to carry him back.

And back he had come.

* * *

"It was the most amazing thing," said Maggie, helping herself to a piece of toast. "I kept feeling I knew that face from somewhere — you know, the portrait of the pretty lady in the white lace gown over the mantle in my room upstairs. But I just couldn't figure it out, and it frustrated me. I fell asleep with the question on my mind. Yet this morning when I awoke, I had the answer just as if someone had whispered to me in middle of the night."

Olivia smiled but said nothing.

"So tell us," said Alexander. He loved her morning face, fresh and natural and still slightly crooked from sleep.

"Do you recall, Alexander, the first day we met when we were driving to Uncle Liam's gallery? You told me your great great grandmother's name was Bisby? You remarked how odd it would be if it turned out we're cousins."

"I did?"

"Actually it was your great great *great* grandmother, dear," said Olivia to Alexander. "The name 'Bisby" first occurred in our family in the early 1800's. Let's see, that would be William and Fannie Bisby whose daughter, Meg, married your great great great grandfather Cyrus Thornheart, the man who built this house. They had a daughter, Annette Bisby Thornheart, who lived just a year, and a son, Cyrus II. *His* son was Cyrus III, whose son Cyrus IV, was my father-in-law, the gentleman with the disapproving look up there on the stair landing." She laughed, breathless from her recitation. "He was very stern — Cyrus IV — very strait-laced, a deacon of the church who disapproved of frivolity and was suspicious of anybody who laughed out loud or appeared to be having a good time.

"As children we were all terrified of him. I must admit, the prospect of having Mr. Cyrus (as everyone called him) for a father-in-law gave me pause about marrying into the Thornheart family."

Olivia giggled girlishly, her color high. "Then at our wedding reception, Carter spiked his father's punch—just enough to loosen the old boy up. I shall always cherish the picture of my mother, herself bit reserved, teaching Mr. Cyrus the 'Charleston'." She wiped her eyes. "By the way, my Carter's middle name was Bisby."

"And my sister Charlotte's," added Alexander, "but you still haven't told us about the lady upstairs."

"I'll do better than that," Maggie said and hurried out of the dining room. A moment later she was back, bringing with her a heavy gold chain from which hung a ruby-studded locket in the shape of a heart.

"This has been in my father's family for generations," she said. "He gave it to my mother just before he died."

"What was *his* name, dear?" asked Olivia.

"Colin. But mummy told me everybody called him 'Fitz' because his middle name was Fitzhugh."

Maggie wedged her thumbnail beneath the delicate clasp of the locket and opened it carefully, laying it on the tablecloth. "You see—on one side, my great, great great grandfather Fitzhugh Bisby and on the other, his sister Mary Margaret. Ta daa, the same face! I've always felt a fondness for her since it is after her that I am named."

"Of course!" exclaimed Olivia. "Cyrus once told me there was a brother named 'Fizzy'—short for Fitzhugh. How wonderful! You two are, indeed, cousins—of a very distant sort." She gave Maggie's hand a squeeze.

"Cyrus who?" asked Alex.

"What? Did I say Cyrus? How silly of me. I meant Carter, of course."

Crimson camellia blossoms nodded to each other as a cardinal ornamenting a holly branch trilled in assent. A warm and agreeable winter afternoon.

Alexander whispered in her ear. "May I have this dance?"

"But, of course," said Sam Gray with an elaborate curtsey. The champagne lace of her gown complemented her tawny skin, framing her face and drawing his eye down the length of her arm. As she placed one strong hand in his, he noticed that her fingernails, usually square and utilitarian, were tapered and polished a pale, translucent mauve.

He led her down a corridor of white poinsettias to the corner of the garden where a string ensemble played "The Anniversary Waltz." When the music swelled into "Stardust," they joined another couple on the tiny flagstone dance floor. Alexander pulled her close, and for a few moments they moved together silently. An uneasy dancer, Alexander marveled at the confidence Sam inspired in him as if her own natural grace transferred by osmosis through her hand to his. He drew away and looked down into her face, catching an expression he couldn't fathom.

"You're beautiful."

"And you, sir, look especially dashing."

"Thank you. You like the uniform?"

"Very much. A tuxedo suits you, pardon the pun."

"How'm I doing?" He whirled her dangerously.

"Quite well, actually. Especially for a man who's just been handed a life sentence." She laughed wickedly, then sobered. "I was remembering our first dance together—at Tim's party last spring—and thinking how time telescopes events. Absolutely dizzying. Sometimes it takes all my concentration just to keep my balance."

"I know the feeling." He tightened his arm around her back. "I love you, old friend."

"And I love you."

"Before this party's over, I'm going to find a way to tell Derek Bisby what a short-sighted ass he is."

Sam smiled up at him. "You needn't bother. He already knows. I told him so myself just before I left for the States." She rose on tiptoe to kiss him lightly on the cheek. "Now go dance with your wife."

"Wife." Alex smiled at the sound. "What a peculiar notion!"

* * *

Lucy washed her hands and began arranging slices of fruitcake onto a china platter. Why Miss Charlotte had insisted they serve this nasty stuff Lucy didn't have a clue—especially since a three-tiered wedding cake had been delivered that morning.

"Put this over on that little side table near the fountain," she said, handing Jonas the platter, "and save room on the main table for the good stuff. I don't guess there's gonna be a big rush for fruitcake since we got us ham and turkey and other food folks actually eat." She swiped a paper towel across her forehead. "And while you're up there, Jonas, count the champagne bottles, will you? If there's less than ten, I gotta call Ganem's for another delivery. Lordy, my feet feel like they been fried on a griddle. Get outta here, cat, or you gonna get squashed for sure!"

* * *

Jonas signed "J. Bates" on line twenty-four and exchanged the man's UPS clipboard for a long, narrow package postmarked Ireland. Something inside shifted with a slight clink.

"Looks like a rifle," said Jonas with a grin. "I hope it ain't from the I.R.A."

The delivery man chuckled. "Sounds like quite a party going on."

"Wedding reception. I think it's gonna last all night."

The gift tables were already overflowing, so he leaned the carton against one end. What comes in a box like that? he wondered. Skis? Not long enough. Fireplace tongs? A fishing rod?

* * *

Maggie wiped the kiss marks from her cheek and checked her reflection in the powder room mirror. Damn freckles. Why couldn't she be gorgeous just this once? Why did it matter that she wasn't? It didn't, really. She knew Alexander loved her, freckles and all. And tonight they'd be off on a wonderful adventure, the start of their new life together.

"I'm not worried," she told the other Maggie, "that he's out there dancing with a beautiful blonde." She dropped her voice an octave. "Of whom he has had carnal knowledge." She stuck out her tongue, then opened her mouth wide and massaged her smile-stiffened cheeks. "I'm never going to do this again," she promised. "One wedding is enough."

She pulled the pins from her crown of flowers and carefully lifted Auntie O's fragile veil from her curls, relieved to see she had not snagged its French lace. The gown was her mother's and would have fit perfectly a month ago. Now it was a bit snug in the waist. Maggie smiled, thinking of the tiny creature with beginning eyes, their little secret tadpole curled around itself like the anchovies on the hors d'oeuvres tray. Thank God, the morning yuks were nearly behind her. Soon they'd have to tell their family members, none of whom would ever believe the truth — that this child was planned, scheduled, the result of a conscious decision made by both its parents. The only surprise had been the ease with which it was conceived.

"You were our very best idea," she imagined explaining to her son. "On Monday we wanted you, and on Tuesday — there you were. Were we good, or what?"

* * *

"Alexander's aunt is delightful, don't you agree, Julian? It's as if I've known her all my life. Makes me feel much better about the children's decision to live in America — but, oh, I will miss them!"

"Grace, darling, they'll only be a day away. You can

see them whenever you wish. We'll invite them to join us in Switzerland next month if you like," said Julian.

"No!"

"Of course we will. You know how Maggie loves to ski."

"No! She mustn't."

"Why ever not?"

"Never mind why not. She just mustn't, that's all."

* * *

The box was so securely taped that Derek had to fetch a knife from the kitchen. Together he and Alexander pulled off the wrappings while the other guests gathered around to watch.

"It rattles," said Sam. "I hope whatever's inside didn't break in transit."

Alexander handed Maggie an envelope tucked inside. She opened it and read aloud:

Dear Maggie:

How could you up and marry that paint-splotched imposter when you could have had the likes of me? Inside you'll find a bit of Irish trash so you'll not be forgetting your old friend

Tim

A moment before the box was opened, Sam knew. Hadn't she, after all, helped Tim scout for scraps, watched week after week as he worked the metal with his torch, seen him emerge from his welder's mask, sweating and exhausted? Gradually the project had begun to take shape — a graceful piece added here, a slight elongation there for the sake of proportion —

but Tim was never satisfied. She had left for America before seeing the finished product, not knowing he intended it as a wedding gift. Yet here it hung from Alexander's hand, a delicate, chromed wind chime that gathered the light — from the window, from the Waterford chandelier above, from Maggie's eyes — and sent it forth with music.

* * *

"What are you driving these days?" asked Harold Horner.

"Excuse me," said Beau Harris waving to an imaginary friend. "I need to have a word with someone."

* * *

If she had to listen to Farley tell the one about the Rabbi and the myna bird one more time, she was going to forgodsake scream! Charlotte clamped her smile in place and edged through the crowd to the front parlor. Back straight, chin high, up the stairs on the toes, glide. Even after twenty years, she felt the dictionary balanced upon her head, imagined Miss Paul's critical eye assessing her posture. She wondered how her former dancing instructor had fared in a world without white gloves and the fox trot.

She sat on the edge of the bed in Alexander's old room and rocked back and forth, trying to loosen the knot of anger that twisted her insides. She could still hear Miss Paul's warbley voice: "Gently, dear. Don't be so emphatic about everything. And cross your ankles, Charlotte, not your knees. This time when your partner asks you to dance, offer your hand palm down, and don't forget to look him in the eye."

All her life people had been trying to make her into someone she wasn't — especially Aunt Olivia. "Just because you think something, dear, you needn't always say it. And must you always win? You'll find you have more friends if you learn to lose gracefully once in a while."

What was the point of the game if she didn't try to win? She fingered the afghan at the foot of the bed, the same one her mother used to wrap up in to sit in front of the fire, nodding over a book, her reading glasses slipping down her nose. As Charlotte buried her face in its soft folds, she could almost smell Abigail's perfume.

She stood at the open window, breathing in the sweet tang of camellias in bloom and listening to the tinkle of glass and laughter from the garden party below. Criminal to waste such a splendid house, she thought. Then, with a flutter of excitement, she thought about the mistletoe berries, and a slow smile spread across her face. By this time tomorrow Hibiscus House could be hers.

* * *

The crash of shattered china caused laughter and conversation to stop as all eyes turned toward the fountain. Nearby a small table had somehow overturned, strewing shards and bits of fruitcake across the flagstones. Alex righted the table and stood looking in dismay at the mess. What in the world could have happened?

Then Jonas arrived bearing broom and dust pan, the band launched into "Georgia On My Mind," and the party chatter resumed. Just a minor glitch in an otherwise perfect afternoon.

* * *

From the corner of the garden came a drum roll, causing voices to hush once again and eyes to turn.

"Friends," began Olivia, "dear friends." She clasped her hands in front of her. "This is truly a wonderful day for the Wades and the Thornhearts. Not only has Alexander brought our precious Maggie into the family, but—joy of joys—the two of them have decided to settle here in America. Nothing, *nothing* could please me more!" Her radiance was contagious. "I want to share this happiest of moments with you as I present them with my gift. Alexander? Maggie? Come over here, darlings, for just a moment."

No one but Alex noticed the tremor in Olivia's fingers as she placed a small, silver box in his hand. He hesitated a moment, then lifted the lid and withdrew an ornate brass key. An array of emotions played across his face—curiosity, confusion, comprehension. "But Aunt Olivia—"

"Now you just hush and listen to me!" she said. "This big old house is too full of ghosts for an old lady. Hibiscus House needs noise and toys and girls and boys—" She laughed, delighted with herself. "When your great great great grandfather Cyrus Thornheart built Hibiscus House, he promised his wife—Maggie's ancestor—that it would remain the family home down through the generations. If I were to allow it to be used for any other purpose, he'd haunt me the rest of my days!" Everybody laughed.

"But Auntie O, we can't—"

Maggie gently pushed Alexander aside. "We thank you from the bottom of our hearts," she said. She wrapped her arms around the old lady and kissed her on the cheek. "But Mary Margaret Bisby Thornheart would haunt *me* if we turned you out. Old Cyrus made sure there was plenty of room for us all," she said. "We can only accept this wonderful gift if you'll promise to stay right here." Before Olivia could remonstrate, Alexander signaled to the orchestra and led her to the dance floor.

Had he glanced toward an upstairs window, he would have seen his sister's ashen face twisted in fury and defeat.

* * *

"He jolly well looks like me in that outfit," chuckled Cyrus. "Alexander has his mother's Thornheart nose, for all his father's legacy."

Olivia stretched luxuriously in the dark and pulled the scented sheet up over her shoulders. "Wasn't it a lovely wedding? The weather, the garden, the music—everything was perfect." She yawned. "How he hated dancing lessons!" she said. "Alex was usually such a tractable little boy, but we waged a real battle of wills over that one! I told him he'd thank me one day. And do you know what, Cyrus? Tonight he did." She wiggled her toes. "I went down to the kitchen to find a vase, and there he was—whirling Lucy around and around—the two of them singing, 'I'll be loving yooo, always . . .'"

Night sounds crept across the piazza and in through the open window—a nighthawk's call, the rustle of the giant magnolia, St. John's bell tower marking the quarter-hour.

"It's time," said Cyrus.

"For what?"

"For me to go."

Olivia sat up. "Go?"

"Yes, go—nullify, evanesce."

"No!"

"But it's what I wish to do, Olivia. I'm tired, don't you see. You can't begin to appreciate how exhausting it is to muster up and manifest like this, although I've become jolly good at it, if I do say so myself. Bear in mind, it was my vow to my wife that forced me into this state in the first place. Tonight, when you gave away the key, my promise was kept—my mission completed. I'm relieved it's finally over!"

"You're spoiling my perfect day."

"Listen to the wench!" he snorted. "You've suffered through ridicule, embarrassment, insomnia, psychiatric counseling, group therapy, self-doubt, and a competency hearing as a result of our association. I should think you'd be right glad to see the last of me."

"I've grown used to having you around." A tear spilled over and slid down her cheek.

"Aye, but you're a different person from the one you were that first night. You were weak and forgetful and living in the past. Our time together has been good for you, Olivia. You're in charge now, and you don't take sass from anybody. You've got a busy household to run, and before long you'll be sewing lace on your grandchild's little things and pushing a carriage in Forsyth Park." He rustled noisily. "For whatever it's worth, you have my affection," he said in a gravelly voice. "And my thanks." She leaned forward, straining to hear. "Hard as it is to admit, old girl, I bloody well couldn't have done it without you."

St. Johns tolled again: One. Two. Three.

Olivia lay listening to her heart, trying to think of something to say. He was right, of course. She felt stronger than she had in years—almost young in fact.

Four. Five. Six.

If Carter had been there tonight, she could have danced the Twist.

Seven. Eight.

It would be wrong for Cyrus to stay—especially now that she really didn't need him anymore.

Nine.

"Goodbye, old dear," she whispered.

On the stroke of ten, the air in the quiet room grew chill, and Olivia snuggled deeper, drawing the covers up to her chin. On eleven the atmosphere shifted. She sensed an expanding, an easing of the air pressure, a brief gravitational lift—and finally, a release.

As the twelfth chime tolled out across the quiet night, Tomochichi sprang onto the bed, circled twice, and nestled in the curve of her knees.

Spirit
Willing

OTHER TITLES BY BONAVENTTURE

When Elvis Meets the Dalai Lama

by Murray Silver

The author of *Great Balls of Fire: The Uncensored Story of Jerry Lee Lewis* recounts his favorite stories of how he started out as a rock concert promoter in the late 1960's and ended up as a special assistant to His Holiness the XIVth Dalai Lama. A magical mystery tour of pop culture spanning the 50's through the 90's, with anecdotes about Jerry Lee Lewis, Elvis Presley, professional wrestler Harley Race, pornographer Gail Palmer, and the Tibetan Buddhist monks of Drepung Loseling Monastery. Never before published photographs throughout!

Hardback, 384 pages.   ISBN 978-0-9724224-4-4

Behind the Moss Curtain and Other Great Savannah Stories

by Murray Silver

Ten true stories not found anywhere else in print. Most of the stories are about the good old days when Savannah was run by gangsters and gamblers, a time when the town was known as the "Independent State of Chatham County." Some tragic, some comic, a few ghosts...but all true! The best book ever written about Savannah.

Hardback, 286 pages.   ISBN 978-0-9724224-0-6

Haunted Savannah -2007 Edition

by James Caskey

Savannah's hostory is filled with plagues, wars, duels and murders... no wonder every site in Savannah has a secret past! Here you will find chilling tales, as experienced and told by witnesses, and authentic photos documenting the existence of energy from another dimension. Most up to date book on the subject today!

Softback, 204 pages   ISBN 978-0-9724224-2-0

Fastened to the Marsh, a Savannah Saga

by Jan Durham

The story traces a family's legacy from arrival of an 18th century indentured servant to the begrudging return of her last legitimate descendant in the 21st century. Through flashbacks, the reader is introduced to a procession of stallwart women who draw their strength from their connection to the rythmic life on the marsh and an unfailing conviction that *what cannot be bested must be borne.*

Coming in July 2007

To order, please contact:

www.Bonaventture.com   Sales@Bonaventture.com

Tel or fax (912) 355-7054